Protecting Cheyenne

Protecting Cheyenne

SEAL of Protection
Book 5

By Susan Stoker

Cover Design by Chris Mackey, AURA Design Group
Edited by Missy Borucki

Manufactured in the United States

Table of Contents

Acknowledgements

Thank you to my awesome Facebook friends who spent a night brainstorming various 'jobs' that Cheyenne could hold. I thought about making her a drywaller, but then decided that wasn't quite right. Ha! Thanks for keeping it real and helping me out with suggestions and helping to make my characters "real."

To Phyllis, my inspiration and model for 911 operators everywhere. Thank you for all your do. Thank you for suffering through your own kind of PTSD. While I've never been there, anyone who has ever had to call 911 to get help, thanks you and is thankful you were there to help them.

For Cathy, Celeste, Beth, Phyllis, Karen, Wendy, Alicia, Mickey, Chris, Mandy and all my other LGBT friends and readers…keep on keepin' on.

Chapter One

"911, WHAT IS your emergency?"

"Is this the police?"

"Yes, this is 911, what is your emergency?"

"My cable went out and I can't get my shows."

"Ma'am, this line is for emergencies only."

"Yeah, I know. This *is* an emergency. My DVR isn't working and I have to see what happens to Toni tonight."

Cheyenne sighed. Jesus, she hated these calls. "Have you tried calling your cable company?"

"Yeah, but they weren't answering."

"What do you want me to do?" Cheyenne was shorter than she probably should've been, but this was an emergency line and she was exhausted. She didn't have the time or patience for this crap.

"Can you see if you can get through to them for me? I need them to fix this now."

"Okay, hold on. Let me see what I can do." Cheyenne put the woman on hold and plunked her head on the desk in front of her. She took three deep breaths then sat up straight again and clicked the caller back on. "Okay, I got a hold of them and they said you should call them back. They'll see what they can do for you."

"Oh my God, thank you so much! I appreciate it."

"Have a good night, ma'am, and I hope Toni is all right."

"Yeah me too! Thanks again. I'll call them right now."

Cheyenne clicked off the phone again and sighed deeply. Working as a 911 operator sounded much more glamourous than it was in reality. Most nights she had at least one or two people calling in with the most ridiculous "emergencies." Technically, she was supposed to report them and give the info to her supervisor, but it was usually just as easy to get the person off the phone, quickly and politely, than try to report them and get them in trouble.

It never made sense to Cheyenne to take up a police officer's time to go out and give a warning to these types of people when the officer could instead be concentrating on finding bad guys or helping people that honestly needed assistance.

Cheyenne turned back to her laptop sitting next to the other computer and electronic equipment on her desk and clicked back on the movie she'd been watching.

Typically, Cheyenne was the only phone operator on duty for her small section. She worked the second shift, which she loved, but she could go hours with no calls at all. She learned quickly to bring something to do, otherwise she'd die of boredom. She wasn't typically a "night" person, but working from three in the afternoon to eleven at night suited her. She could sleep in, do errands in the mornings, and still have time to get to work in the afternoons.

The job was much harder than Cheyenne had thought it'd be when she'd first applied. She didn't mind talking to people. Giving out basic first aid advice was kind of exhilarating; she enjoyed being able to help keep someone alive or even simply calm them down until the paramedics or police officers could get there. Lately, however, Cheyenne had been feeling antsy and discontented. It wasn't until she read an article online about post-traumatic stress, that she understood her feelings.

Every time she answered the phone was potentially a life and death situation. Cheyenne would spend anywhere from three to twenty minutes on the phone with someone, helping them, working through whatever issue they had…only to hang up once the police or paramedics arrived, not knowing what the final outcome was.

Oh, sometimes she'd see a story on the news and recognize the situation as one she assisted with on the phone, but most of the time she had no idea how things turned out. Was anyone arrested? Did anyone die? Were they okay? By the end of each night Cheyenne was so full of adrenaline, that it'd take quite a while to get to sleep when she got home.

Perhaps even worse than the not knowing, was that Cheyenne was lonely. She spent her time at work talking with others, but she never really got to know them. She spoke with people on what many times was the worst day of their life. Only once in the five years she'd had her job, had someone tracked her down to thank her. Once.

Working second shift made it hard to make and keep friends, never mind finding time for romance. She worked five days on and four days off. She wasn't really a party girl and usually didn't go to the bars. She knew people from her station at work, but they typically had opposite schedules than she did, so they couldn't exactly socialize together outside of work.

Cheyenne recalled a conversation she'd once had with her mom. She'd called to try to get some sympathy after a hard day at work where she'd had to try to console a woman who'd found her husband dead in their home. It had been emotional and Cheyenne had cried at the woman's grief after she'd hung up. She should've known better than to try to get any sympathy from her mother.

"I don't know why you get so worked up over people you don't even know, Cheyenne," her mom had scolded.

"Mom, they call me when they need help. Most of the time they're freaked out and just need someone to tell them it'll be okay. That's me."

"But, honey, you're always getting emotional over your job. Why can't you find a normal job, like your sister?"

Cheyenne had just sighed. She knew most people didn't understand what she did or why she did it, but she'd always hoped her family would come to understand and support, rather than mock, her.

She wished she was closer to her sister, but ever since they'd been little, Karen had been ultra-competitive with her. Cheyenne never understood it because she couldn't care less about competing with her sister, but since Cheyenne had been a "surprise" when Karen had been five, she supposed the adjustment of being an only child to being the big sister of a baby, hadn't been a smooth one.

Karen was a paralegal to a criminal lawyer in town and Cheyenne knew her mom loved to brag to her friends about her "successful" daughter. Cheyenne had learned to keep her hurt about how her mom treated her to herself. There was no use trying to change her now, she'd never understand.

The phone rang, startling Cheyenne out of her reverie, and her heart rate immediately skyrocketed. There was no way to tell what kind of situation she'd be trying to help the caller with. She pushed "pause" on her movie, and picked up the phone.

Chapter Two

FAULKNER "DUDE" COOPER stared stonily at the woman behind the counter at the gas station. He was wearing jeans and a T-shirt and was paying for the gas he'd just put in his car, as well as a coffee and six pack of doughnuts. Hell, breakfast of champions it wasn't, but he'd just run ten miles and lifted weights for half an hour. Six measly doughnuts wasn't going to hurt him. He'd pulled his wallet out of his pocket and reached in to pull out a twenty dollar bill. Dude hadn't thought about his hand, he'd gotten used to working around the missing parts of his fingers.

He looked up just in time to see the woman looking at his hand in horror. Dude sighed and held out the bill impatiently, waiting for her to take it.

He should be used to the reactions his hand got, and for the most part he was, but every now and then it still caught him by surprise. Dude's teammates on his Navy SEAL team didn't give a shit about his hand, and their women were just as easy going about it. Thinking about it, Dude realized that not once had any of them acted like his hand was repulsive. That thought was enough to let him ignore the looks, like the one the cashier was giving him.

Just to be perverse, Dude held out his left hand for his change, forcing the woman to once again look at his mangled hand. He smirked at her with a grin that didn't reach his eyes and pocketed the change. Shaking his head, Dude grabbed up his snack and coffee cup, and headed back out to his car.

He stuck the doughnuts under his chin, and opened his door with his now-free hand. Dude snagged the sugary snack from its resting place in his throat and sat down in the driver's seat. He took a sip of the coffee, grimaced at the taste of burnt convenience store sludge that tried to pass itself off as coffee, and started the engine. He drove forward and out of the parking lot.

"I bet she would've acted differently if she knew I was a SEAL," Dude thought bitterly to himself. He shook his head. He was getting more and more maudlin as the days went on. He had to shake himself out of it.

He pulled up outside of Wolf and Ice's house. Ice never failed to cheer him up. The two had met when the plane they'd been in had been hijacked. Ice had smelled the drug in the ice in the drinks they'd been served, and Wolf, Mozart, and Abe had managed to take out the terrorists. Of course the FBI double agent had figured out Ice had something to do with the plot being foiled, and arranged to have her kidnapped and tortured.

After she'd spent too much time in the hands of the terrorists, the team had been able to rescue her, but it had been touch and go for a while. Ice had been Dude's introduction into what real love was. His own family hadn't been the touchy-feely type and he'd always felt as if he'd let them down. His parents wanted him to go to college, but he'd decided to enter the military instead. They'd wanted him to choose the Marines, and he'd gone into the Navy. They'd wanted him to be a doctor, he'd chosen the SEALs. Dude didn't go home much anymore. He only felt awkward and uncomfortable, knowing he'd disappointed them.

Dude left the crappy cup of coffee in the holder in the car and headed toward the front door. He smiled when it was thrown open before he could even knock.

"Faulkner!"

Dude went back on a foot as a blonde dynamo threw herself into his arms. He smiled, and mock-chastised her. "Jesus, Summer, take it easy on an old man would ya? And how many times do I have to tell you to call me Dude?"

"Whatever! I'm not going to use that ridiculous name. I don't care if you were a champion surfer in high school. You are not a 'Dude' and I won't call you that! And you're not old! If you're old, I'm absolutely ancient." It was an old joke between the two of them. "It's good to see you. It's been a while."

"How are you?" Dude asked seriously.

"I'm good."

"No, *how are you?*" Dude used his "I'm in control voice" knowing Summer wouldn't be able to resist telling him what he needed to know. Summer had been through hell at the hands of a serial killer. Dude had been just a second too late, or he would've been the one to have killed him. Wolf had pulled the trigger before Dude or Benny could get their k-bars out and slit Hurst's throat.

"I'm okay, Faulkner. I swear," Summer told him before hugging him again.

"All right, come on, let's get off the front porch and get inside."

Summer grabbed Dude's mangled left hand and towed him into the house. If he hadn't already been rejected that day, he probably wouldn't even have noticed. He marveled at the fact Summer didn't even flinch. She'd never, not once, been disgusted at the sight or feel of his hand. That thought made Dude feel slightly better, and gave him hope that there were other women out there that would feel the same.

They walked into the kitchen where Wolf, Ice, and Mozart were sitting around the table. Summer let go of his hand and immediately went to Mozart. He pulled her into his side and curled his hand around her waist. Mozart kissed the side of her head, and Dude smiled as Summer put one hand around her man's shoulder, and the other curled around his at her waist.

"Hey, Dude. Glad you could make it." Mozart greeted his teammate with honest enthusiasm.

"You know I feel like a fifth wheel around you guys."

"Whatever," Caroline said, rolling her eyes. "We love when you and Kason hang out with us. Just because you're single doesn't mean we don't want you around."

"I know, I was teasing." Dude tried to put sincerity into his words, but was afraid they fell flat when he saw the worried looks in his friends' eyes.

Dude pulled out a chair and settled into it at the table.

"What's for dinner, Wolf?" Dude asked, knowing the man was probably grilling up some sort of meat on his new fancy grill in the backyard.

"New York Strip Steaks for us and grilled chicken for the ladies."

"Awesome, don't want to waste the meat on the women."

"Hey!" Summer grumbled, scowling at Dude.

"Kidding!"

Everyone laughed and relaxed. Dude really enjoyed hanging out with his friends. Somehow they made all his other worries and concerns disappear.

The group spent the rest of the evening laughing and talking about nothing in particular. By the time Dude left, he'd forgotten the feelings of rejection he'd momentarily felt earlier that evening.

Chapter Three

"**J**UST ANOTHER BORING *day in my life*," thought Cheyenne as she pushed her cart around the grocery store. She was in day two of her four days off in a row. She'd slept in that morning and decided to get the grocery shopping out of the way. She hated to cook and usually ate herself out of house and home before forcing herself to go to the store. She lived on packaged food and easy to make processed food. She had no inclination to learn to cook. Cheyenne figured she was somehow missing the "cooking gene" or whatever it was that made other women want to learn how to make delicious meals.

Besides that, Karen was an excellent cook, it was just one more thing her mom used to measure her against her sister, and Cheyenne always came out the loser. Cheyenne mentally shrugged. It wasn't as if she had anyone to cook for anyway.

She wished she had a best friend, or even a good friend to hang out with, but after Cheyenne graduated from high school, she lost touch with the few friends she did have. Oh she went out with people from work when they could all get off work at the same time, and she'd honestly call them her friends, but she didn't have that one special woman to hang out with that a lot of other people had. She'd always wanted a best friend, but she was happy with the casual friends she did have.

Once again Cheyenne thought about her job and how it should be more fulfilling than it was. She thought saving people's lives would be exciting and rewarding, but all it turned out to be was stressful and boring at times. *I'm 32 years old, I should be doing something interesting with my life. I should be traveling, or even married by now.*

Cheyenne's life depressed her. She lived in Riverton, California, near the Navy base. She saw men and women in uniform every day. She'd once thought about joining up to "see the world" as all the recruiting posters claimed, but she really was too much of a coward to go through with it. Besides, there was no way she'd be able to pass the physical tests. She wasn't fat, but Cheyenne didn't think she'd be able to do even one pull up, and running was completely out of the question.

Cheyenne found military men fascinating. She assumed it was because she didn't really know any, but like many woman, she found a man in uniform irresistible. She wasn't living in a fantasy world though, she knew they could be mean and ugly, just like any other person. She saw the stories in the newspaper all the time about killings and beatings and such that happened on and around the base, not to mention manning the phone lines and hearing and getting help for domestic incidents that sometimes involved members in the military, but it didn't keep her from fantasizing about men in uniform in general.

There was one man that she saw on a semi-regular basis at the grocery store who immediately came to mind when she thought of the Naval Base. He wasn't usually in his uniform at the store, but she always knew it was him. He was fairly tall, had dark hair and he was built. Cheyenne was ashamed to admit that she'd stalked him around the store one day, watching as he filled his cart with healthy food, nothing like the pastries and processed crap she always bought.

He was always polite to the people around him. He even helped her get a can of something off the top shelf once and smiled at her as he'd done it. Cheyenne had beamed the rest of the day like a schoolgirl. She didn't know his first name, but she knew his last name was Cooper. It was sewn onto the front of his uniform. She'd only seen him wearing it on one occasion, but she knew she'd never forget it. He filled it out in all the right places. She had no idea what kind of job he did in the Navy, as she didn't know what all the patches on his uniform meant, but it honestly didn't really matter to her. Ever since Cheyenne had seen him in the store, she refused to shop anywhere else, just in case she'd run into him again.

Cheyenne found it interesting to people watch as she went about her day. Since she had to sum up a person after only a brief conversation at work, she'd gotten really good at it. One of her favorite things to do was imagine what people's lives were like just from looking at them. Cheyenne looked around her in the grocery store…it wasn't very crowded, which was good because she preferred to do her shopping when there weren't hordes of people around.

There was a lady walking in front of Cheyenne in the produce section. She was wearing three inch heels and a skin tight dress that barely covered her backside. *I don't know how people wear those things. I bet she's an undercover police officer, she's just gotten off duty where she tried to arrest men soliciting prostitutes and is getting some food before she heads home.* Cheyenne looked at a college aged man standing at the meat counter. *I bet he's having a barbeque today and is trying to decide what to buy to grill for his buddies.* Cheyenne continued her daydreaming as she wandered around the store. She wasn't in a hurry, because the only plans she had that day were to go home and finish the book she'd started the day before.

Cheyenne started up the frozen food aisle and noticed five men standing around near the pharmacy. As the store was pretty empty, they really stood out. They didn't have carts with them and they were dressed all in black. About the time her brain processed the fact that something wasn't right, she heard yelling, and the men all pulled out pistols from somewhere hidden in their clothing. Cheyenne stood frozen. When she'd wished for more excitement in her life she really hadn't meant something like this! She started inching backwards to get out of the aisle and out of sight of the men, but one noticed her and started down the aisle toward her pointing the gun directly at her.

DUDE LAUGHED AT his friends. They loved eating at *Aces Bar and Grill.* It was their go-to place for both drinks and food. They'd tried to get everyone together at least once a week. The bar might not be big, and it certainly wasn't a chain, but the food was delicious and, perhaps most importantly, wasn't overrun with tourists.

If Dude was honest with himself, he knew it didn't matter where they ate every week. He loved his friends and their women. He loved to rib his teammates as much as he could.

"You guys are pathetic!" Dude teased, rolling his eyes at the other men on his SEAL team. "Seriously, you never want to go out anymore, you stay home all the time. You're all a bunch of fuddy duddies now that you have women. I'm impressed you even left your houses at all today."

"Hey, you're just jealous," Mozart shot back, laughing at his friend.

Dude laughed with his friends, knowing Mozart was right on so many levels. He looked around and was thrilled to see the happiness on his friends' faces. Their women were perfect for them.

The men were startled when the sound of Wolf's cell phone pealed. They watched as he answered it and they all sat up straighter when they saw his muscles get tight. A phone call could mean nothing more than a telemarketer had somehow gotten a hold of Wolf's unlisted number, or it could mean they were about to be shipped out to an undisclosed location.

Dude watched as the four women around them also tensed, waiting to hear what the news was.

"Right, yeah, I'll get him on it. Thanks." Wolf hung up the phone and turned to Dude. Not beating around the bush he stated urgently, "Possible bomb threat inside the grocery store on Main Street here in Riverton. They're asking for an ordinance expert."

"I'm on it." Dude stood up quickly, already thinking about what he might find. The local police department would sometimes call on the military when they needed extra help. Their commander had no qualms in reaching out to the team when he knew they'd be able to help.

"Let us know if you need anything."

Dude raised his hand in acknowledgement of Wolf's words, then he was gone.

CHEYENNE HAD NEVER been so scared in her life. She'd seen movies and read books where the heroines were brave and smart-mouthed the bad guys. Somehow it had always worked out for them though. Cheyenne didn't think smart-mouthing back to these scary men would help her, or anyone else around her, in any way shape or form. They were mean, and somehow Cheyenne knew they wouldn't hesitate to pull the trigger and kill any one of them.

Apparently they wanted to rob the pharmacy in the back of the grocery store of their drugs, but unfortunately, their plan had failed. Three SPs, Naval Shore Patrols, happened to have been in the store at the time they tried to rob it. Guns were drawn and a stand-off ensued. Cheyenne had been trapped in the store, along with two other women, and the five gunmen. They'd hauled them all to the back corner of the store.

The SPs had managed to get all of the other customers out of harm's way and out of the building in the chaos that had ensued once the gunmen had pulled out their weapons. It seemed like forever had passed since they'd taken over the store, when in actuality it had only been about an hour and a half. The gunmen were mad and desperate. Cheyenne could tell they were getting more and more anxious as time went on. Occasionally she'd hear mumblings of a loudspeaker outside the building.

The two women trapped with her were hysterical. They were both pretty young, maybe in their early twenties. Each time one of the gunmen would look their way, they would plead with them to let them go, that they had families, that they had children, that they were married...whatever they thought would sway the gunmen into showing mercy and letting them go. When that didn't work, they just sat huddled together and cried.

While Cheyenne was also scared to death, she didn't figure that crying would do much good. These guys were obviously high on some kind of drug and they only cared about getting away. Since there were five of them, Cheyenne knew there was no way she and the other women would be able to "make a break for it," anyway. They were stuck until this standoff was over, however "over" occured.

She thought about her coworkers. Had anyone called 911? Had one of her coworkers answered the call and sent out for more help? Cheyenne wished with all her heart she'd never stepped foot in the grocery store that day. That's what wanting to eat got her. What she'd give to be sitting in the control room at work and organizing the rescue from the outside. She'd never thought much about being a victim herself. She was always the one helping others, she never considered that *she'd* be the one needing help.

Cheyenne was brought back to her present situation when one of the gunmen, the biggest and meanest looking, stalked over to their corner and snarled, "Today's a good day to die."

This, of course, got the cashiers even more hysterical than they already were. He laughed with a cruel low grunt. Cheyenne knew he was enjoying making them scared. She just sat there dry eyed and tried to tamp down her terror.

"Here's the deal, ladies," the scary man sneered. "We can't get out of here until those cops get out of the way, and they aren't going to do that unless we make them, that's where you come in."

Cheyenne sucked in a deep breath, knowing whatever he had in store for them wasn't going to be good.

"Since I'm in a good mood today…" Cheyenne couldn't help but snort under her breath. She apparently hadn't been quiet enough with her scorn because the man glared at her nastily before continuing. "I'll let you all decide who gets to deliver my message to the cops outside."

Cheyenne could practically feel the nervous energy coming off of the cashiers. She knew they were dying to be the ones to take the message out of the building. But Cheyenne wanted to know what the catch was. There was no way this evil man was just going to let one of them walk outside and go free. They were their ticket out of there and Cheyenne knew it.

The gunman walked away, but called back to them, "Stay put bitches, I'll be right back with the message."

As soon as the man was out of earshot, the cashiers started arguing with each other.

"I need to get out of here," the blonde said.

"No way, *I* should be the one to deliver the message, you aren't married, no matter what you told him," the other woman argued back.

Their voices got louder and bitchier as they argued with each other.

"Yeah, but I have to be here to take care of my mom, you know she's not doing well," the blonde shot right back.

Cheyenne sighed. She didn't bother joining in their argument. She was glad the two women hadn't turned on her yet, they weren't even *considering* her to be the one to get out of there with the message. She was basically invisible to the women. But that was okay, Cheyenne was single, had no husband or kids…essentially she was expendable.

The women stopped their arguing as the man came back toward them holding a box. Cheyenne shuddered, knowing that whatever was in that box wasn't good. They'd all assumed he'd come back with a piece of paper with the gunmen's demands written on it. No one had expected a box.

The man carefully put the package on the floor and turned toward them, with his hands on his hips as if daring them to defy him. "Here's the message…it's a bomb."

Cheyenne gasped and shrunk back from the innoc-uous looking box on the floor, just as the two cashiers did the same thing.

"The message is, that if they don't let us out of here, we'll blow up this bomb and everyone in the store. Shrapnel will blow for fucking miles…anyone in the vicinity of the building will die…holes punched throughout their body," his voice trailed off as he laughed. Then he glared at them all again and said, "You have three minutes to choose who will take the message outside. I'm sure it won't be hard to decide. After all, whoever gets to take it, will be free." He again laughed, but Cheyenne couldn't hear any humor in the laugh. He stalked off to converse with his fellow gun-men, leaving them there to figure out who would be the one to carry the deadly bomb outside to the cops.

Cheyenne turned to the two women; they all just looked at each other. Predictably, the cashiers started to cry. Cheyenne wasn't very far from crying herself, although she willed the tears away. If she was going to die, she wasn't going to do it sniveling.

Whispering, Cheyenne turned to the two women. "It sucks, but he's right, whoever takes this outside will be free."

"But, it's a bomb," the blonde woman croaked, not able to tear her horrified eyes away from the box sitting in front of them.

"What if it's not?" the other woman said. "I mean, what if they just want us to *think* it's a bomb to scare us, but it's really only a piece of paper in there?" Cheyenne thought about it. The girl was right, he could be trying to scare them and it wasn't anything.

"Are you crazy enough to take a chance on that?" the blonde whispered.

The other cashier's shoulders slumped. "Hell no."

"Well, I know I don't want to risk it. These guys are crazy. I'm not sure I'd trust them to know how to build a bomb, nonetheless build it sturdy enough to withstand being carried through the store."

Unfortunately, Cheyenne agreed with her.

As if realizing she was there for the first time, the cashiers turned toward her. "What about you?"

"Uh…" Cheyenne couldn't think of anything to

say, but the blonde didn't give her a chance anyway.

"I don't see you wearing a ring, so you aren't married. Do you have kids?"

Cheyenne shook her head honestly, knowing where this was going.

"Then you have to do it. We have families, people who depend on us."

When Cheyenne just stared at them, the dark haired woman joined in with the pleading, but at least she was nice about it. "Please," she begged.

Finally after another moment, knowing it was probably the best decision, Cheyenne decided to just go with it. If all it took to be free from this nightmare was a moment of danger to walk that damn box out the door, it'd be worth it. "I'll do it," Cheyenne croaked to the other women. "I know you both have families. Hopefully it won't come to anything; we'll just have to believe that." The women nodded and didn't say anything.

The gunman stalked back over to the frightened women and demanded, "So? Who's taking my message outside?"

Cheyenne stuck her chin up and said simply, "Me." She really didn't like the wicked smirk that came over the man's face as he turned to her.

"Then get up, bitch, I gotta prepare my gift for the cops."

Cheyenne slowly stood up, regretting with every fiber of her being what she was about to do. She knew this wasn't going to end up well for her. She just knew it.

DUDE PACED OUTSIDE the grocery store. He hated waiting. So far no one knew much about what was going on inside the building. The SPs that were in the store when the robbery had started had done a great job in getting almost everyone out, but they said there were still some civilians inside. He wasn't sure how many, and the gunmen weren't really talking except to say if they weren't allowed to leave, then they would set off a bomb and blow everyone up. That was where he came in. Everyone knew he was the best, all he needed was a chance to diffuse the bomb, but no one knew if they would have that chance.

Dude heard one of the police officers say, "Look!"

He turned and watched through the plate glass window as two women walked across the front of the store toward the front door. They were holding each other and walking quickly. There was no sign of any of the gunmen. Had they sneaked out? Was that even possible? He watched as the women exited the store and crept toward the line of police cars.

"Stop right there," one of the police said through his bullhorn. "Turn around, put your hands on your head and get down on your knees." The women did as he asked. Four police officers cautiously peeled away from the line of cars they'd been standing behind as cover, and approached the women with their guns drawn. They grasped them by their hands, which were behind their heads, had them stand, and practically dragged them back behind the police cars.

Dude listened in as the cops quickly interrogated the women on the spot, trying to get more intel as to what the hell was going on.

"How many gunmen are there?"

"Five."

"What kind of firepower do they have?"

At the blank look from the women, Dude rolled his eyes as the officer explained that he wanted to know what kind of guns the bad guys had.

"Oh, they each had a little gun, but the leader guy had like, two of them, and a long gun too," the blonde explained, wringing her hands dramatically.

"Did they let you go? How'd you get out of here?"

This time it was the dark haired woman that answered. "They wanted one of us to take a message out here to you guys, but then the big guy said the message was a bomb. The other lady said she'd do it and the guy took her in the back. They left us alone, and we decided to get the hell out of there, we didn't want to get blown up. We ran toward the front of the store and by the time they noticed us, we were too close to the door, so they had let us go. But they're pissed, that's for sure."

"So there's only one other hostage inside?"

At the nods from both women, the officer asked again, "You're sure?"

"Yeah, positive," the blonde said frantically nodding. "Yeah, you heard her say the message they wanted us to take out here to you was a bomb? Neither of us wanted to take it, and we have family, there was no way we could've done it. The other lady volunteered."

Dude clenched his teeth. Volunteered his ass. More likely the two young women flatly refused to do it and the other woman was left, literally, holding the bag.

Dude was getting itchy. He wanted nothing more than to get his hands on that bomb...if there was one. At this point he truly didn't know if anything the gunmen, or the hysterical women, said could be believed. There were no doubts that everyone in the area was in danger, however. The gunmen were unstable, armed, and getting more and more desperate. They wanted out of the store and Dude knew they'd do anything to get what they wanted. He wondered what their next move would be.

They didn't have long to wait.

CHEYENNE SWALLOWED HARD. She was boring Cheyenne Cotton...the woman that nothing exciting ever happened to, how had she ended up with a fucking bomb duct taped to her body? She thought they were going to make her *carry* the bomb outside...to show the cops they were serious, but the gunman had different plans. He'd made her hold the bomb against her stomach then started taping it to her. Going round and round and round her with the tape, until she couldn't move. *Then* he flicked a switch near the bottom of the device and taped her up some more. He'd activated the bomb and taped the whole thing so much Cheyenne couldn't see any of it through it all. But she could feel it ticking against her chest. She was going to die. Damn it all to hell.

DUDE WATCHED AS five men inside the store walked toward the front door. He wished like hell his team was there. He hadn't had time to call Wolf once everything started happening, and now all the police with their guns drawn were making him really nervous. Dude had no idea where the supposed bomb was in this cluster fuck, just that his hands were itching.

All of the police had their weapons pointed at the men as they walked to the front of the store and could be seen on the other side of the big plate glass windows. There was no way they were getting out of this. The men were walking in a triangle/rectangle formation with a woman at the point, shielding them. They were pushing her ahead of them as they walked. When they got to the front door it was opened a crack.

One of the men yelled out, "You let us walk out of here and we'll let her go, you don't, she'll die, along with all of you, courtesy of the bomb she's currently fucking wearing!"

Dude turned his attention to the woman. He hadn't really been focused on her as the men came into sight, he'd been concentrating on escape routes and trying to ascertain what type of fire power the men had. Looking now, Dude couldn't see anything on the woman other than miles of silver tape. It looked like they had used multiple rolls to mummify her in the heavy tape. Dude honestly couldn't tell if there was a bomb under all that tape or not, the gunmen could be bluffing. But Dude knew they couldn't treat the situation as anything *but* a bomb threat, for their own safety and that of the woman who was as white as a ghost and being held tightly by what would have been her upper arm if it hadn't been encased in tape. If the look on her face was anything to go by, there most likely was a bomb under all the silver tape holding her still. She looked freaked and terrified out of her mind. She obviously knew, as did the officers all around him, that the odds of her getting out of whatever fucked up situation this was without getting hurt…or killed…were extremely low.

As soon as the man who'd yelled the threat shut the front door, all hell broke loose. Apparently the snipers had gotten the approval to take the gunmen out. There were five men inside the store, but there were also more than enough snipers to go around. Not only were they near a Navy base where SEAL snipers were plentiful, the local SWAT team had their own cadre of the deadly officers as well.

The standoff had been going on for well over four hours Dude knew everyone wanted it to end. Glass went flying in all directions. He *knew* the snipers were good at their jobs, but he hoped like hell they hadn't missed and hurt the woman. The situation was chaotic and shooting through glass always held a modicum of danger. The woman was an innocent bystander, a terrified bystander. Dude had only gotten one quick look at her, but he'd been impressed at how she'd been holding herself together.

She was scared, yes, but she hadn't screamed, hadn't tried to wrestle herself out of the arms of the gunmen, and amazingly hadn't been crying. If nothing else, Dude hoped the sniper's bullets hadn't hit her to reward her for her stoic behavior in the face of extreme danger.

CHEYENNE FLINCHED AS the glass in front of her

shattered. She immediately ducked as low as she could go, which wasn't too far since she was bundled up in the tape. As she crouched on the floor, she was more than aware of the ticking of the bomb against her stomach. More glass shattered around her and Cheyenne felt a spray of wetness against her face and back. One of the gunmen sagged against her and she lost her balance, falling toward the front door of the store. Cheyenne couldn't throw out a hand to stop her forward momentum and ended up wedged against the glass that hadn't been shattered by the gunfire by the weight of at least one of the men who'd been terrorizing her for the last few hours.

Cheyenne quickly glanced around, taking in the broken glass, the blood on the floor, and the bodies of the five men around her. Damn, she was amazed she was still alive. Every one of the five men who'd held her hostage was lying dead on the ground. She'd always been impressed with the skills of snipers, but she was even more so now seeing their prowess up close and personal.

She took a deep breath; and knew she was losing her mind when she was thankful she could still feel the ticking of the bomb against her body. Falling hadn't set it off, thank God, but it was still active and ticking away. She had no idea how much time she had before it exploded, but Cheyenne figured she was going to die.

She didn't see any way to get the damn thing off of herself without it blowing up, but she didn't want any innocent people to die with her.

Cheyenne managed to use the shaky glass in front of her to brace with her shoulder and push herself upright. She scooted away from the body of the man leaning against her back, the man she'd thought of as the leader of the gang. His eyes were open and staring sightlessly toward the ceiling. He looked almost as scary dead, as he was alive…just without the maniacal smile he'd shown her as he'd taped her up. She stepped to the left, around the bodies of the other men littering the tile at the front of the store…stepping around the broken glass and rapidly spreading blood pools, and walked backwards toward the aisles in the store. Cheyenne kept an eye on the front parking lot, willing all the cops and rescue personnel to stay away as she made her way away from all the commotion in the parking lot, away from the people so she didn't kill them as the bomb blew up.

AS SOON AS the dust settled, Dude was running toward the store along with about ten of the other officers who'd been waiting and watching the front of the grocery store. He didn't have a gun, but he wasn't concerned, he was there for the bomb, the other officers would take care of peripheral safety. Time was of the essence. It always was when bombs were involved.

Dude heard the officers shouting to someone, "Stop, don't move," as they moved forward. He saw the bodies of the gunmen on the ground by the door, but didn't see the woman who'd been trussed up like a mummy. When Dude got further into the store and looked down one of the long aisles, he saw her, still bound up in all that tape, backing away from the officers as they moved toward her.

They were all yelling at her to stop, to surrender. She was shaking her head and saying "No, no, don't come near me, you don't understand."

The woman was as pale as the tiles under their feet, and her dark hair, which had been in some sort of ponytail or braid at one point, had mostly come loose and was hanging limply around her face. She had blood sprayed on her face and right side and she was stumbling a bit as she backed away. Dude couldn't stay quiet anymore.

"All of you halt," he ordered in his best Alpha voice. The officers stopped at once, guns still drawn and mostly pointed at the ground instead of at the bound woman, but she kept backing away from them all, ignoring the command in his voice.

"Let me through," Dude urged as he elbowed himself to the front of the line of officers. He turned his back on the woman and spoke to the twitchy men in front of him, "If that *is* a bomb she has strapped to her under all that tape, I need to get to it. I can't do that if she keeps backing away. Give me a moment."

The officer in charge nodded, knowing exactly who Dude was and why he was there. "You have two minutes, she might be in on it with them. We won't put our guns down. We've got your back."

Dude nodded, not agreeing with the officer about the terrified woman being in cahoots with the gunmen, but knowing he had to work quickly to get to the bottom of whatever was going on. He knew the local cops were used to working with the military, but they were on edge and their adrenaline levels were sky-high. He'd learned to control his adrenaline high through his training. "Just let me talk to her," Dude told the officer curtly and turned back toward the woman.

She'd steadily backed herself halfway down the snack aisle and hadn't stopped while he'd momentarily stopped to talk to the officers. Dude stepped toward her, leaving the line of officers behind him without a second thought. He knew they'd split up and were coming in behind him and probably around the next aisle to cut off her retreat. It's what he and his team would do if they were in this situation. Dude knew he had to figure out what was going on before that bomb went off and they were all killed.

"Why don't you stop and talk to me, it's okay, it's

over, the men are dead, you're okay." Dude kept his voice low and soothing, but put just a hint of the man he was behind his words with the hopes she'd respond to the subtle command.

Cheyenne just shook her head, didn't they understand? She *was* the bomb for crying out loud. What was he doing? Why was this man coming toward her? She didn't listen to his words, she just wanted to get away from him and hide somewhere in the back of the store. She figured she could find a place to hole up so when the bomb exploded it didn't kill anyone…well, anyone but her. But holy cow, from what she could see through the tears in her eyes, the man in front of her was gorgeous. She didn't want to be responsible for killing him. Hell, he probably had a family, a wife, kids…she couldn't kill him.

She kept backing up. Cheyenne could barely see through her unshed tears. She would not cry, she would not cry, she had to get these people out of here. Through her panic, Cheyenne heard something behind her, she turned and was horrified to see two police officers at the end of the aisle. They'd cut her off. Shit, they were all going to die after all she'd tried to do. She turned sideways, so her back was to the shelves and shut her eyes tightly. A couple of boxes of something fell off the shelf behind her, but she didn't bother opening her eyes to see what it was. At this point, making a mess was the least of her worries.

"Ma'am," Dude said again, seeing her stop after spying the officers at the end of the aisle. "Can you hear me? Look at me and talk to me, tell me what's going on."

Cheyenne opened her eyes and looked more closely at the man who'd followed her down the aisle for the first time. He didn't have a weapon, but was standing about ten feet from her. His hands were at his sides, palms out, showing her he was no threat. But Cheyenne knew he was close, too close. If she could just get him to back off, maybe he'd somehow survive when the bomb went off.

"Please," she croaked, then cleared her throat and tried again. "Please, you have to get out of here....just go…"

Dude saw her trying to hold her composure together, and his impression of her rose. "You know we can't do that, these police officers have to make sure you're all right and that you aren't an accomplice." Dude saw her eyes widen in surprise. He'd purposely tried to shock her, so she'd stop and listen to him. "Yeah, I know, seems unlikely to me, but they're just doing their job, no matter what you or I say to them. Why don't you help us and we'll all get out of here and have some lunch." Dude tried to get her to smile just a bit.

It was obvious his attempt at humor fell flat, when

she flung her words at him. "No, you have to go, all of you. I'm not 'in' on anything." Cheyenne gestured to her chest with her chin. "This bomb is going to blow up and kill everyone." Her voice dropped and she changed tactics, begging now, "Please, just go, I don't want anyone to die."

Dude suddenly understood and his stomach clenched with respect. She wasn't trying to get away; she was trying to *protect* them. He hadn't been sure there even *was* a bomb, but now that he was closer to her, Dude could see a lump in front of her body that could be anything, but with the way she was acting, it probably was exactly what the bad guys had said it was. If that bomb *did* go off, there was a good chance many of them *would* die, or at least be badly hurt.

Dude abruptly turned away from the woman who was obviously scared to death, and to the officer in charge who'd followed at a close distance behind him down the aisle.

"Get your men out of here, *now!*" Dude bellowed. "That bomb strapped to her chest could go off and we need to clear the area. I've got this."

The officer took one look at Dude's serious face, and ordered his men back.

Dude turned back to the woman as the officers backed away from the aisle on each end, and made their way toward the front of the store. "Okay, they're leaving, now will you let me help you?"

The woman resumed her relentless retreat away from the front of the store now that the officers weren't blocking her way.

"No, you have to leave too, don't *do* this to me." Cheyenne looked at the man in horror, suddenly recognizing him as "Cooper," the military guy she'd semi-stalked in this exact grocery store. Oh my God. It was even more important he just let her go. *He* couldn't die. Not him.

Dude ignored her words and strolled steadily toward her and said again in the low commanding voice that, in the past, women had a hard time disobeying. "Look, you're wasting my time. I'm a bomb ordnance technician, if anyone is going to prevent that bomb from going off and killing you, me, and anyone else nearby, it's going to be me, so for God's sake stop backing away from me and let me help."

Cheyenne stopped, surprised by his words and the tone of his voice, and let the man get closer to her. As he came up toward her, she whispered, "I don't want you to die."

"I'm not going to die if you let me take a look at that bomb. If you don't, then we'll both *definitely* die because I'm *not* leaving you." Dude was slightly surprised at the words that left his mouth. It wasn't like him to be reckless, or to let himself be swayed by a woman, but there was something about the bravery and self-sacrifice of *this* woman that touched him deep inside. She had been one hundred percent honest with him, he could tell. She'd honestly rather just lock herself away in a back room and let herself be blown up, then allow anyone the chance to help her, just in case she couldn't be helped. It wasn't acceptable in Dude's eyes.

Dude reached out and took her arm, or what he thought was her arm...it was hard to tell since it was under miles of duct tape, and steered her toward the back of the store. "You're right though, we have to get away from the windows up front, come on."

Cheyenne let herself be led away from the front of the store and the officers and onlookers that had congregated there.

Dude led the woman into the small room behind the meat counter. He helped her lean against one of the butcher tables where the meat was packaged and stared at the tape around her body, trying to work it all out in his head before he tackled it physically.

"Talk to me," Dude said to the trembling woman now standing in front of him. "Tell me what they said as they put this on you and how it's attached."

Cheyenne didn't like the fact this man was here with her and in such horrible danger, but she didn't know what else to do. She really didn't have a choice. He seemed to know what he was doing. She couldn't get the tape off herself, and she certainly couldn't disarm the bomb. She took a deep breath and did as he ordered. Maybe, just maybe, she could give him something that would help get the damn bomb off of her.

"He didn't say much. He asked me to hold it in my hands, which I'm still doing, and they started with the tape. Once I was mostly taped up, he flicked a switch near the bottom, and then taped me up some more. I can feel it ticking against my body."

The man hadn't looked her in the eyes since they were in the aisle; he was wholly focused on the contraption and her mummified body, as if he had x-ray vision and could see under the tape.

"I'm afraid I might hurt you trying to get some of this tape off," Dude started to tell her, looking up in surprise when the woman let out a sharp laugh.

"I think the tape will hurt less than the damn bomb going off...go ahead, do your worst."

Dude looked up at her for the first time. She was splattered with blood, a tear had escaped from her right eye, and she had what looked like the beginning of a black eye, but she was still standing there in front of him, with a bomb strapped to her chest, and making a smart ass comment. Amazing.

"By the way, my name is Dude."

Cheyenne sighed, did it matter? Yes, she thought it *did* matter. "Dude?"

Knowing she'd probably ask, Dude had purposely given her his nickname. "Yeah, it's a nickname. When my buddies in boot camp heard I'd spent most of my time in high school surfing, instead of studying, the name stuck."

"What's your real name?"

"Faulkner. Faulkner Cooper. What's your name, hon?"

"Cheyenne Cotton," she told him softly.

"Well, Cheyenne, let's get this thing off of you." Dude pulled a chair over toward her and sat down to work.

After ten minutes of Dude trying to get the tape removed, without either hurting her, or prematurely triggering the bomb, Cheyenne said urgently, "Promise me something."

Dude didn't look up but replied immediately and honestly, "Anything."

"If you can't get this thing off, you'll get the hell out of here."

Dude *did* look up at that. "Sorry, Shy, I can't promise that, anything but that. Ask me to take you out for dinner, ask me to come to your house and rake up your leaves in the fall, hell, ask me to kiss you, I'll agree with no complaints. But leave you? Not gonna happen."

Cheyenne started a bit at the nickname he'd used. No one had ever shortened her name before. It felt intimate. She liked it, but now wasn't the time or the place to acknowledge it. She ignored his other words, figuring they were said to make a point in the heat of the moment. "You don't know me," Cheyenne continued desperately. "You don't owe me anything, I'm a nobody. Look at you, you're gorgeous, and you're an honest-to-God hero, I know you are, you should *not* give up your life for mine. I'm just not worth it."

Cheyenne took a deep breath and babbled on, not giving Faulkner a chance to say anything. "I don't have any close family, I'm not married, no one will miss me. I just *know* that you have loved ones who'd be mad as hell if you got killed. Look at you, you survived one bomb already, don't let this one kill you, I couldn't stand it." Cheyenne's voice trailed off.

Dude didn't stop fiddling with the tape or with the bomb after her passionate speech, he just kept his head down and continued with what he'd been doing. Cheyenne shifted nervously, if he was pissed she'd mentioned his hand, too bad, maybe it would make him leave.

"How do you figure I've survived one bomb already?" Dude asked, not addressing her other points. They weren't worth him giving them the light of day. But he was honestly curious as to her train of thought and how she'd figured out he'd survived an explosion in the past. Dude also figured it'd distract her and let him keep working. She was pretty persistent, something he usually admired, but right now he wanted her concentrated on something else.

"Well, um, your hand…I figured since you're here now trying to get this damn bomb off of me and you said you were a bomb…order…whatever…and well…I just thought…" Cheyenne trailed off, not sure what she even really wanted to say.

"Well, you're right. I *do* do this for a living. I'm a bomb ordnance technician in the Navy, among other things. I can't say I'm a hero, but I have a whole team of men that depend on me being good at my job. And, hon, I *am* good at my job. Damn good. The bomb that took three of my fingers notwithstanding, I know what I'm doing. I'll be damned if those yahoos get the best of me."

Cheyenne was silent for a moment, but couldn't stay that way. This was too important. "Please, Faulkner…"

Dude cut her off, not letting her finish her thought. "Hush, you're ruining my concentration," he told her not harshly, and not truthfully. He was one hundred percent focused on the bomb in front of him. Dude was sweating now and he was just getting past all the tape to the actual bomb underneath. He could see Cheyenne's hands now, and he had access to the bottom switch, just where she'd told him it was. Dude was in luck, it looked like a fairly simple switch, but he couldn't be certain.

He wouldn't put Cheyenne's life, or his own, at risk on a hunch. He needed to uncover a bit more of the bomb itself to be sure.

Dude was impressed with Cheyenne. He knew she was scared to death, but she was holding herself together. He didn't know too many people, soldiers included, that would've done what she did…try to get everyone else out of harm's way. He told her so as he continued to work.

Cheyenne shook her head. "That's not true," she told him.

"Tell me how the other two women were able to sneak past five armed men and get out while you were being strapped to this bomb?" Dude asked her, already figuring he knew the answer, but wanting to see if Cheyenne would come clean.

Cheyenne was silent.

"That's what I thought," Dude said after a moment. "You volunteered, didn't you? Then you created some sort of distraction…" He took the time to slowly reach up and brush her darkening eye gently before turning back to the contraption taped to her belly, and finished his sentence, "…that allowed them to escape out the front door."

Cheyenne sighed. Faulkner was pretty smart, but Cheyenne hadn't been able to simply to be led like a lamb to the slaughter to have the bomb taped on. She'd struggled just enough to make sure the men's attention was all on her, and before the biggest guy had hit her, she'd caught the other women's eyes and gestured nonverbally toward the door, hoping they'd understand. They did. They'd snuck out as the men were subduing her. A black eye was worth it to Cheyenne.

"Just like I told you, I don't have anyone, they do, it was better this way." Cheyenne looked at the top of Faulkner's head as he continued to try to get to the bomb. She watched as sweat trickled down the side of his face. He wiped it off with his shoulder and kept working. Cheyenne wished her hands were free so she could wipe the sweat out of his eyes for him, but that was crazy. No, it was creepy, she'd just met the man for goodness sake.

Cheyenne couldn't believe this was "Cooper"...the man she'd daydreamed about for weeks and had followed around this very store once. He was just so gorgeous...she certainly hadn't dreamed *this* was how he'd be touching her though. The touch of his hand on her face had been short, but it'd sent shivers shooting down her spine nevertheless.

Cheyenne looked at Faulkner's mangled hand to distract herself. She meant what she'd told him. She knew he was a hero, and while his hand wasn't pleasant to look at, Cheyenne also knew what someone looked like made no difference as to the person they were inside. That hand was pure magic as far as she was concerned. If it was going to get this bomb off of her, she didn't care what it looked like. He was missing half of his middle three fingers on his left hand, but she noticed it didn't slow him down at all. He was still able to use what was left of his fingers to maneuver around the bomb. She wondered what it would be like to feel his hands on her...

Dude worked in silence for a bit longer before Cheyenne told him out of the blue, "I know you, you know."

That surprised Dude and he took his attention from the bomb for a second and looked up briefly and met Cheyenne's eyes before dropping his gaze and concentrating on the device again.

"Really?" he said. "Have we met?" Dude didn't know if he would remember her or not. She wasn't exactly looking her best at that moment, but what he saw, he liked.

Cheyenne nodded and told him, "I guess we haven't really *met*, met, I've *seen* you around."

Dude nodded, gritting his teeth, he was getting to a tricky part. "Ah, it is a small town," he told her absently.

"It was actually here, we were both shopping, we passed each other in an aisle, and you helped me get a can down from the top shelf. I told you I could probably use the bottom shelf to step up and get it myself, but you insisted, for my own safety, that it was your duty to keep me out of danger...." Cheyenne's voice trailed off and she mentally smacked her forehead in consternation. She hated her tendency to sometimes ramble. "I know you don't remember, that's okay, I'm sure it's just your nature to help people." They were both silent as Dude worked and merely nodded to acknowledge her words.

Dude took a deep breath. It was now or never. He thought he'd discovered the line that was connected to the C4 that was strapped to her chest. He could see the bomb also had at least two pounds of nails inside it. If it went off it *would* send shrapnel flying. They would certainly be dead, just as the gunman had said. He didn't want to think about what Cheyenne's body, or his own, would look like if those nails went flying.

Dude looked up at Cheyenne. "I've reached enough of this damn bomb so I can disarm it. Are you ready?"

Cheyenne looked into his eyes. He didn't look nervous, he was calm and matter of fact. She tried to calm her heartbeat. If he was confident enough not to quake in his boots, she would be too. "I'm ready," she told him with far more bravado than she felt. Before he moved, she quickly asked, "Do you mind if I close my eyes?"

Dude chuckled, feeling amusement for the first time since he'd arrived on scene and had seen this woman. "I'd close mine too if I could," he softly told her with a smile.

Cheyenne squeezed her eyes shut. She was still all mummified in the duct tape, still couldn't move much, but she felt lighter just by having him there.

Dude cut the last wire and waited.

Cheyenne's eyes flew open to see Dude looking up at her expectantly. "What?" he asked her urgently. He didn't *think* there was a secondary trigger, but it could be possible.

"I don't feel it ticking anymore," Cheyenne told him. "Was that it?"

Dude smiled and stood up, scooting the chair back as he did. He swiped his forehead with his bicep, removing the sweat that had built up there. "That was it. Let's get out of here," Dude told Cheyenne, reaching for her arm to guide her out of the store.

Cheyenne shook her head and pleaded with him. "Please...please take the rest of this tape off me now, before we go out there."

Dude studied Cheyenne critically. She'd held up extraordinarily well. He'd worked in some situations where he had had to knock civilians out because they were hysterical and wouldn't let him concentrate on working. This woman had not only stood there without moving, but she'd kept her calm at the same time. Dude really didn't want to hurt her though, and he knew removing the tape *was* going to hurt.

"Cheyenne," Dude started to deny her, but she interrupted him, frantically struggling against the bonds of what was left of the tape around her body. Now that the bomb was removed it was as if she couldn't stand the feeling of being bound.

"Please, Faulkner, I can't move...I can't breathe...need to get out of this...I..." she stopped and panted a bit and looked at the floor. Cheyenne took a deep breath and stopped moving, obviously trying to get herself under control. "Never mind, I'm okay. Let's go."

Dude couldn't help the feeling of rightness that went through him at the sound of his real name coming from between this woman's lips. Oh, Ice and the other women used his name all the time, but somehow it sounded different coming from Cheyenne. Dude stopped her from stepping away from him with a hand on her tape covered arm. She hadn't asked for much of anything during the whole ordeal, Dude figured he could give her this. "Calm down, Shy. Let me see what I can do. Lean back against the table."

Cheyenne braced herself back on the table while Dude reached over and grabbed a large pair of scissors that had been sitting on the table behind them. He regretted not having his k-bar knife with him. Since he'd been at *Aces* with the guys, he hadn't bothered to put it in his pocket before heading out for the night. Dude made a mental note to start carrying the damn thing with him wherever he went from now on.

He started at the bottom of the tape roll at her side and slowly snipped his way upward. The tape didn't move as he snipped, as it was stuck to her arms as well as to her clothing and the remnants of the bomb. Dude then went to her other side and did the same thing. She wasn't exactly free, but it was a start. He continued snipping around her on the tape until he'd gotten most of it cut.

Finally Dude looked at Cheyenne and said, "I don't want to hurt you, but taking this tape off your arms *is* going to hurt."

"I don't care," Cheyenne urged. "Just do it."

She flinched when he ripped off the tape on her left arm. Cheyenne knew that most of her arm hair had probably gone with the tape, but she was afraid to look. She scrunched her eyes closed as she heard Dude take a deep breath.

"How bad is it?" Cheyenne asked him softly.

Dude took a deep breath and tried to calm himself. He didn't know what kind of adhesive was on the tape, but it'd been strong. There were places on her arms where some of her skin looked like it had been taken right off with the tape. It was red and blotchy, and extremely painful looking. You wouldn't know it to look at Cheyenne though; she stood there stoically, waiting for his answer.

"Well," Dude started. "It's not too bad. I tried to be careful, but it's gonna be painful for a while. Please don't make me do that again," he said, referring to her other arm.

Cheyenne sighed. How could she refuse him when he'd done so much for her already? What was left of the skin on her arm where the tape was removed hurt bad, but she figured pragmatically that it would've hurt a lot more if she'd been blown up into tiny pieces. "Okay, thank you for at least loosening it up."

They looked at each other for a moment, each lost in their thoughts. They'd just been through a pretty intense experience.

Cheyenne looked at Faulkner and liked what she saw. She thought he was older than her, but not by much. He had dark hair, and dark eyes, which were looking at her as if she was the only other person on the planet. Cheyenne had always loved a man in uniform, and this man wore his well. She didn't know what he was thinking, but she kind of liked the intense look in his eyes as he peered down at her.

Dude looked down at the woman standing in front of him with respect. He didn't like to admit it, but he was used to women being weak, his teammates' women notwithstanding. The women he dated certainly were. Part of that was their submissive sexual desires, but it was more than that. Dude was used to taking charge and controlling those around him, but he hadn't had to do much to take charge with Cheyenne. She was strong, and did what needed to be done, regardless of her feelings or what she wanted to do.

Dude couldn't have stopped his hand from moving up to her hair to smooth it away from her flushed face if his life depended on it. "You're an amazing woman, Cheyenne Cotton." Dude lingered a beat as he ran his mangled hand over her hair to her shoulder, then he said, with a touch of regret, "Let's get out of here."

Dude carefully steered Cheyenne toward the front of the store. He put his hand on her lower back and they started walking to the front door. Cheyenne stopped when she saw the crowd that was outside the store. Of course there were police officers and military men around, but she also saw a lot of TV vans and cameras. She should've realized the media would be there, but she'd been worrying about other things...namely living through the last hour or so.

Cheyenne took a deep breath and said quietly to the man standing patiently next to her, "I know it's asking a lot...but....." she paused, nibbling her lip, trying to work up the courage to ask a huge favor of the strong military man standing next to her.

"Yes?" Dude prodded her gently.

"Will you hold my hand as we go out there?" Cheyenne looked up at him. "I know it doesn't mean anything, but I don't think I can face all of that," she gestured toward the front of the store with her head, "right now." Cheyenne could feel her face flame. She was so embarrassed, but she'd never felt as alone as she did looking at the mob she'd have to go through when she walked out the door.

Dude felt something shift deep inside of him. She was covered in grime and blood, she still had tape wrapped around most of her, her arm looked like it was horribly painful and all she wanted was someone to hold her hand. It was such a little request, but in his eyes it was huge. Women didn't usually ask him for favors, they waited for him to dole them out. Dude's respect for Cheyenne, in the face of everything she was feeling and going through, rose dramatically, and it was already pretty high.

He must have hesitated a bit too long before answering, because Cheyenne suddenly shook her head, looked down and mumbled, "Never mind, it was stupid anyway. Let's go," and started toward the door.

Dude caught her right hand in his left before she could take two steps and before he even thought about the fact she'd have to hold his injured hand. He'd made it a point never to hold a woman's hand with his injured one. Ever. "Cheyenne," he said softly, "it's not stupid. There's nothing I'd like better than to hold your hand as we face the lions together. Come on." The words were nothing but one hundred percent truth. Dude wasn't above lying to get cooperation from someone, but he wasn't lying now. The feel of Cheyenne's fingers in his was something Dude knew he'd never forget. She wasn't disgusted, she wasn't repulsed, she simply tightened her fingers around his and held on for dear life, as if she couldn't feel the scars and missing fingers on his hand. On the outside, she looked calm and composed, but the tight grip on his hand proved it to be a façade.

Cheyenne gripped Faulkner's hand tightly in hers, swallowed hard, put her chin up, and took a deep breath. She started for the front door, hand in hand with the larger than life man next to her and knew, even with everything that had happened to her in the last few hours, she'd never forget this moment. Holding this man's hand, letting him support her in that small way, meant more to her than any other gesture he could've made. She'd needed him and he hadn't hesitated to step up to the plate. Not only step up, but not make her feel bad for asking in the process.

Cheyenne blocked out the questions from the re-porters, the police officers' demands, the lights, the noise…all of it, and concentrated on holding on to Faulkner's hand and following him wherever he wanted to lead her.

Chapter Four

CHEYENNE SAT IN the lobby of the emergency room waiting for her taxi. The walk from the front of the store to the ambulance was a nightmare she didn't want to think about. The only good part was Faulkner's strength as he helped clear the way for her. At one point she'd been jostled hard enough that she would've fallen to the ground if it hadn't been for Faulkner. He'd taken his hand out of her own and wrapped his arm around her waist and curled her into his body. Cheyenne hadn't even been ashamed to lean into him and let him help her.

With everything she'd been through in the last few hours, it had felt so good to be held tight and safe against Faulkner's side and let him deal with making sure they made it through all the people safely. He'd helped her over to the ambulance and made sure she'd settled into the gurney without any issues. Once she was sitting and stable, Faulkner had kissed the top of her head briefly and squeezed her hand one last time. The last Cheyenne had seen of him was as he'd backed out of the ambulance. He'd given her a smile and a half wave before the doors shut in his face.

She'd spent the last three hours in the hospital. She'd given her statement to the police about what had happened, at least what had happened from *her* viewpoint. The nurses had removed the rest of the tape, which had been more painful than Cheyenne had thought it would be, and had both arms gooped up with lotion and antibiotics and who knew what else.

The first time Cheyenne had looked in the mirror, she'd been shocked. She was a mess. She was splattered with blood and her hair was hanging limply against her head. Fortunately a nurse gave her a pair of scrubs she could change into and let her brush her hair. Cheyenne supposed she was lucky, but the only thing she could think about was getting home and into a nice hot shower.

The problem with that was she wasn't supposed to get her arms wet for the next twenty four hours because of the bandages and the antibiotic mixture they'd smeared on her arms. The nurses had helped as much as they could in trying to get the blood out of her hair, but Cheyenne knew until she had a shower, she wouldn't feel clean.

She sighed. Cheyenne hadn't seen Faulkner since he'd helped her into the ambulance and squeezed her hand. She didn't expect to see him again really. After all, he was just doing his job. He'd go home and probably shoot the shit with his friends about what a crazy day he'd had, and then continue on with his life, just like she would…except first she had to *get* home.

Since her car was still in the grocery store parking lot, Cheyenne had to call a taxi. It really was pathetic that she didn't have one person she felt comfortable in calling and asking to come get her. There was no way in hell she was calling her mom or sister. They'd never let her live down her bad luck. A shitty day would just get worse if she involved either of them. Eventually she'd call and explain everything that had happened, but it'd have to be on a day she felt better able to deal with them. And that day certainly wasn't today.

Cheyenne knew she was a loner. She didn't really mind, except for times like this. She could've called one of her friends from work, but she hated to rely on other people, and besides, they weren't really the kind of friends that she felt comfortable calling out of the blue to pick her up from the hospital of all places. So, she'd simply called a taxi and now was waiting to go home. Home to her lonely apartment. Cheyenne still had two days before she had to go back to work and she planned on crashing in bed and sleeping for one of those days, then she'd take the longest shower known to man, and *then* get herself together and back into the routine of her life.

Cheyenne laughed out loud, making the little old lady sitting in the hospital waiting room look at her disapprovingly. She still had to get some food. She'd been at the grocery store that afternoon for a reason. She had some cans of cream of mushroom soup and salad dressing, and that was about it. *Screw it. I'll order in until I can I get back to the store.* Cheyenne knew she'd never shop at the grocery store she'd been held hostage in again, even if it was where she'd first seen Faulkner. And even if it was a popular store for other men in uniform. It wasn't that she thought she'd be taken hostage again, it was just…she didn't know. She wasn't comfortable with the thought of entering the store again.

The taxi finally arrived outside the automatic doors. Cheyenne made her way outside, verified the car was there for her, and climbed into the backseat that smelled slightly of body odor and cigarette smoke. After giving directions to the taxi driver, Cheyenne put her head back on the seat, deliberately not thinking about how many germs and nasties might be lurking on the head-rest, and closed her eyes. She felt weird. The pain killers the doctors had given her were obviously doing their job because she wasn't in any pain, but they also made her a bit woozy. She probably shouldn't be driving once she got to her car, but it wasn't too far to her apartment from the parking lot of the grocery store. She'd be extra cautious. She'd be fine. She always was.

DUDE COULDN'T STOP thinking about Cheyenne. She had to be the bravest person he'd met in a long time. Her actions reminded him a lot of Ice's. Hell, all of his teammates' women for that matter. Cheyenne had faced what happened to her with courage and she hadn't panicked. From the first time Dude had seen her backing away from the officers trying to keep them from harm, to the last look he had of her smiling bravely at him as he left her in the ambulance, she'd been grace personified.

He didn't want to leave her, but Dude knew he had to give his statement to the local cops and get back with his CO. He'd spent a good hour going over what had happened inside the store with Cheyenne and what he'd done and seen. Since Dude wasn't related to Cheyenne, there was no reason, or really any excuse, for him to go with her to the hospital.

The press had been relentless. Dude knew it was their job, just as it was his job to give a report of what had happened, but this time was different somehow. Each time they asked the police department's representative probing questions about Cheyenne and where she lived and what she said and what she thought and what she did, Dude just wanted to rail at them and tell them it was none of their damn business and to leave her alone. Cheyenne was a grown woman, she could handle herself...she didn't need him. But there was something about her that made him want to wrap her in his arms and protect her from the world anyway.

THE TAXI PULLED up in front of the grocery store. "*Was it just this morning I was here?*" Cheyenne thought ruefully. Seriously, it felt like it'd been days since she'd walked into the store intent on buying enough to fill up her pantry so she'd be good to go for a good long while.

Cheyenne painfully eased out of the back seat after paying the driver. As the taxi pulled away, she started walking toward her car. She'd parked near the back of the lot that morning, as was her habit, to try to get a little extra exercise. As she approached her car she heard the sound of a vehicle pulling up behind her.

Feeling extraordinarily cautious after everything that had happened, Cheyenne quickly turned and watched as a huge pickup came to a stop and Faulkner hopped out. Cheyenne looked at him in confusion. What was he doing here? She looked around to see if anyone else was there that he was meeting. There was no one else. The parking lot was deserted, it was only the two of them.

Dude eyed Cheyenne as he neared. She looked perplexed to see him. She also looked tired…and adorably cute. She was wearing blue scrubs from the hospital, no doubt because her clothes were ruined. They were big on her, and it looked like if she moved the wrong way, the pants would fall right off of her. There were dark smudges under her eyes, which made her black eye even more prominent, and both arms were bandaged from wrist to elbow, and probably beyond, but Dude couldn't see because of the scrubs she was wearing.

"Hi again," Dude said softly as he came to a halt in front of Cheyenne.

"Um…Hi." Cheyenne said haltingly. "What are you doing here?"

Dude laughed and looked her in the eye. "I started thinking about how you probably drove to the store today, and since you were taken to the hospital in the ambulance that somehow you'd have to get back here to get your car. I wanted to meet you at the hospital and see how you were doing and give you a ride, but when I called, they told me you'd already been discharged. I'm sorry I missed you."

Cheyenne looked at the man in front of her in confusion. "You called? Why would you do that?" she asked, not thinking about how rude it sounded until it was too late. "I…I…mean," she stammered, eager to make sure Faulkner didn't take offense.

Dude chuckled. "I know what you mean, Shy, and

to be honest I'm not sure why…I just wanted to be sure you were okay and to see if I could help you in some way. What did the doctor say?" He gestured at her arms with his chin.

"Uh, okay, well, I'm okay. They just bandaged my arms to make sure they wouldn't get infected or anything. They're covered in some slimy horrible goo that makes me want to scratch. I'm not supposed to get them wet, which is ridiculous because the goo is gross and I feel disgusting after everything that happened today. I don't have any food in my apartment, which isn't surprising considering I was in the damn store in the first place this morning. My food is probably still sitting in my cart in the middle of one of the aisles, and I'm hungry, and I don't know if I can eat anything because the pills they gave me are making me feel really weird."

Cheyenne's words faded in the air around them and she immediately closed her eyes. Holy shit, had all that crap really just spewed out of her mouth? She was mortified.

"Aw, come here, Shy." Dude felt his heart melt a bit more at her words. She was adorable. Whatever drugs they'd given her were obviously making her much more talkative than she probably normally was. He'd known a few sailors and marines who reacted the same way to painkillers. They'd talk and talk and talk seemingly without any filter. It was a hell of a lot cuter on Cheyenne.

Without waiting for her to move, Dude took a step toward her and pulled her into his arms. He relaxed as Cheyenne melted into him. He'd been half afraid she'd rebuff his attempt to soothe her. Dude heard her sniff once, then felt her bury her nose into his neck. Her breath was warm against his skin and Dude tilted his head just a bit until he was touching her with his cheek.

"You smell good."

Dude smiled. That wasn't what he thought she'd say. She was constantly surprising him.

"Thanks." Dude stood in the dark parking lot holding an amazing woman and realized he didn't want to let her go. "Can I take you home?"

"I need my car."

"I don't think you should be driving. I don't know you all that well, but I imagine if you were in your right mind you never would have told me all of that other stuff. Am I right?" He felt her nod reluctantly against him and smiled. "Okay then. I'll take you home. I'll arrange for your car to get to your apartment." Dude knew he could call any of his teammates to come and get it and drive it home for her.

Cheyenne was too tired to argue or even protest. It felt so good to be taken care of, she couldn't remember a time when someone had offered, or who she allowed, to take care of her. At that moment Cheyenne would've probably agreed to anything Faulkner said.

She startled when he spoke again, "I gotta hear you say it's okay, Shy."

Cheyenne forced herself to look up at the man holding her. She looked into his eyes and saw nothing but sincerity. "Okay, but if you're really a serial killer can you please kill me quickly? I've had a really bad day." Her words came out softly, but with one hundred percent honesty.

Dude laughed out loud and brought his hand to Cheyenne's cheek. "Painkillers really loosen your tongue, don't they?" He asked rhetorically. "Don't worry, Shy, I promise I'll get you home in one piece. You're safe with me."

"I *feel* safe with you. I don't know why or how, but I do. Thank you, Faulkner. Seriously. I know you probably have better things to do than lug my ass around. But I appreciate it. I do. Really."

Dude pulled back and kept a hand around Cheyenne's waist, and steered her toward his truck. "I know you do, hon. Come on, let's get you home. We don't want you turning into a pumpkin. Do you have your keys?"

"Yeah, my purse was delivered to me at the hospital by one of the cops when he came to get my statement. I have no idea how they found it in the chaos of the store, I sure as hell couldn't have just slung it over my shoulder and pranced out of the store with you."

Dude nodded, glad he wouldn't have to pick the lock to her apartment to get her inside. He would've done it, but it wasn't exactly the first impression he wanted to leave Cheyenne with. He opened his passenger door and helped her sit, then reached over and buckled her in. Dude closed the door and made his way around to the driver's side. He settled into the seat and looked over at Cheyenne. Her head was resting against the headrest and she was turned toward him.

"What is it, hon?"

"You're hot. I'm assuming you know this." Cheyenne sounded like she was imparting some deep dark secret to him.

"Shy…" He didn't disagree, but he didn't agree either. She was extremely charming all drugged up. Dude shuddered to think about her actually driving in this condition.

"Seriously, you *are*. I don't know why you're here though. Did you lose a bet or something? Are your buddies around somewhere ready to bust out and laugh?"

"What?" Dude was getting pissed. Cheyenne couldn't mean what it sounded like she meant.

"Yeah, no one who looks like you has ever taken a second look at me before. I'm just me. You're…well…you're sex on a stick."

Dude didn't even smile at her words. She had to be kidding him. "Hon…"

"No, really. I know I'm not a troll. I'm passable, I actually think I've got great calves, and I like my arms…at least I did before I had the hair completely ripped off of them. Let me tell you, I don't think duct tape is gonna become the new fashion fad anytime soon. But I'm not the kind of woman you probably are with all the time. I bet chicks throw themselves at you. When you go out to the bar I bet you always leave with someone right? Oh shit! I bet you hang out with a gang of hotties don't you? Jesus, You leave a wake of devastation behind you wherever you go, don't you?"

Dude raised his right hand and covered Cheyenne's mouth lightly. He didn't know whether to be pissed at her assumptions, or to be flattered. When she stayed silent, and simply looked at him with wide eyes, he told her, "Cheyenne, first, there's no fucking bet and I'm kinda pissed you'd even accuse me of something like that. I think you're exquisite. Funny. Cute. Interesting. And there's nowhere I'd rather be than right here, right now, with you. Second, yes, I have a group of friends and we hang out, but almost all of them are either married or in a serious relationship. We don't leave a wake of anything behind us, because we only have eyes for our women." Dude didn't even stop to think about what he was saying, that he was suddenly including

Cheyenne in his thoughts and words.

"I hope like hell when you wake up in the morning and the pain pills have worn off you'll remember this conversation and want to hang out with me and my friends. You're like them more than you know."

Dude smiled at the look on Cheyenne's face. She hadn't picked her head up off the head rest, but watched him with serious eyes.

"But you're perfect..." She mumbled the words around his hand and would've said more, but Dude interrupted her.

"I'm not even close to fucking perfect. I'm kinda a slob, I have a tendency to throw my shit on the floor until it annoys me too badly and I have to put it in the hamper. I have a temper, but I'd never raise my hand to you or any other woman. I'm controlling and like to be in charge. And..." Dude held up his left hand, reminding Cheyenne of his disfigurement. "Enough women have told me this is disgusting, or just plain gross, for me to think I'm anything but perfect."

Cheyenne didn't even think. She brought her hand up to his and grasped it tightly and brought it to her mouth. She kissed each mangled stub of a finger as she spoke. "Those dumb bitches don't know what they're talking about. You're perfect, Faulkner. These little scars don't mean dick. Wait, yes they do. They mean a lot. They mean you're a hero. That you've suffered helping our country, helping people out of shitty situations. I don't know what kind of situations, 'cos if you told me, you'd probably have to kill me, but I don't really want to know anyway 'cos I'm kinda a wuss. But if those women rejected you because of your hand, they're complete morons. Seriously." Cheyenne closed her eyes, still feeling dizzy, and at the same time wanting to concentrate on the feel of Faulkner's skin against her own, and brought his hand to her cheek, missing the look of endearment on Dude's face.

"Your skin is so soft, except here." Cheyenne rubbed her face against his scars. "It's rough and where your fingers were, the skin is raised and bumpy. It feels so good against my skin. It's like a massager. I can only imagine what it'd feel like…"

Cheyenne stopped abruptly and Dude could see her blushing. Was she really going to say what he thought she was? "Go on, Shy, this I want to hear."

Cheyenne let go of his hand, but Dude continued to brush his fingers against her cheek.

"Uh, anyway, those women were idiots."

"God, you're fucking sweet."

Cheyenne opened her eyes and saw the intensity in Faulkner's. She wanted to close her eyes, the cab of the truck was filled with a weird vibe, but she couldn't.

They stared at each other for a moment before Dude's hand left her cheek and went behind her neck.

He pulled her toward him and kissed her forehead and stayed close with his lips resting against her for a moment, before pulling away.

"Let's get you home, Cinderella, before the clock strikes midnight."

"I love that story," Cheyenne sighed dreamily.

"Why doesn't that surprise me?" Dude said absently as he started up his truck and headed out of the parking lot.

Cheyenne giggled at his words and fell silent.

"Where am I going, Shy?"

"To my apartment."

"Yeah, I got that, but where is that?"

"Oh. Shit. These are some crazy drugs."

"Yeah." Dude waited a beat, then reminded her of his question.

"Sorry. I live at Oak Tree Apartments on Copper and Fifth."

"I know where that is. Thanks, I'll get you there. What apartment?"

Cheyenne turned to him again and teased, "Are you *sure* you're not a serial killer?"

Dude laughed at her again. "I'm sure."

"Okay, I'm 513 in building four."

"Close your eyes, Shy, I'll get us there in a bit. You rest and I'll wake you up once we've arrived."

Cheyenne did as Faulkner said. She closed her eyes

again and relaxed into the seat. "Thank you for the ride, Faulkner. I didn't have anyone else to call." She couldn't stop the words.

"You're more than welcome. Now shush."

Cheyenne smiled, but didn't open her eyes. Her head was swirling too much to fall asleep, but it was heavenly to be able to relax and not worry about anything for a while.

Chapter Five

CHEYENNE OPENED HER eyes and groaned. She knew exactly where she was and everything she'd said and done the night before. She would've been happy if she could've forgotten it all, but she wasn't so lucky.

Last night, Faulkner had pulled up to her apartment building and helped her out of the car. He'd half carried, half walked, her up to her apartment and taken her keys out of her hand when she couldn't seem to get the key into the lock.

Cheyenne was embarrassed Faulkner had seen her apartment. She was a slob, as he'd claimed to be. She knew it, but it was her little secret. Not anymore. She wasn't going to agree with him when he'd talked about how he didn't like to pick up his clothes from the floor. It was somewhat manly and macho when a man did it, but when a woman had a messy house, somehow it was pathetic. Faulkner had opened her door and laughed outright at seeing her mess. Cheyenne had tried to explain when she was home from work she just never felt like cleaning or picking up around her apartment, but he just laughed off her explanations.

"The two of us together would be a mess. But at least I know you aren't perfect now, Shy."

Cheyenne had looked at Faulkner as if he had three heads. "Of *course* I'm not perfect, Faulkner. *You're* the perfect one."

"I think we've had this conversation once already. Come on, let's get you to bed."

He'd led her into her bedroom and pulled back the covers. He'd tucked her in, scrubs and all, kissed her on the forehead again and whispered, "Sleep well, Shy. I'll see you tomorrow."

Cheyenne hadn't thought much about it then, she'd been too tired and frazzled from the drugs coursing through her system, but now, in the light of day, it was freaking her out. Faulkner would see her today? Had they made plans and she didn't remember? Cheyenne didn't know if she was ready to spend time with Faulkner...normal time together that was. Without bombs, bad guys, drugs and her being a damsel in distress. She figured he'd get as far away from her as possible, especially after her diarrhea of the mouth last night. Cheyenne buried her head into her pillow and groaned, remembering how she'd actually told him he probably hung out with a gang of hotties. Who said things like that? Darn drugs.

Cheyenne sat up, ready to get out of bed and tackle the shower, when her bedroom door opened and Faulkner strolled in.

What the freaking hell?

Cheyenne pulled the covers back up her body until she clutched them under her chin.

"Good morning, Shy. I hope you feel better this morning?"

Cheyenne could only stare at Faulkner in stupefaction, and nod.

"Words."

Cheyenne had forgotten that about him. Faulkner liked to hear verbal confirmation of his questions. "I feel better."

"Good. I made you some breakfast, we can eat after you shower."

"Breakfast?" Cheyenne could only stare at Faulkner in bewilderment. "I don't have anything to eat in my apartment. I'm pretty sure that was one of the four hundred and fifty four things I blabbed to you last night, that I now wish I hadn't."

"You've got food now. I called Fiona, the wife of one of my teammates. She went shopping this morning and brought over a shit ton of food. It should be enough to last you for a while."

"Fiona?" Cheyenne tried to shake herself out of the

weird dimension she felt like she'd fallen into.

"Yeah, Fiona. Now, come on. Get up. Let's see about removing those bandages. We'll see how they look and if I think your arms look good enough, you can shower. You can do that after the bandages are gone."

Cheyenne tilted her head at Faulkner, but did as he asked. She swung her legs over the side of the bed and sat on the side.

Dude put a hand under her elbow and helped her stand. When Cheyenne had her legs firmly under her, he backed away and waited for her to make her way to the bathroom, which was connected to the little bedroom.

Cheyenne walked in front of Faulkner into the bathroom.

"I'll give you a minute to take care of business, then I'll be back to help you with those bandages."

Cheyenne thought she couldn't have been any more embarrassed than when she'd remembered what she'd babbled last night to the gorgeous man waiting for her in her bedroom, but she'd been wrong. She hurried through using the toilet and brushing her teeth and was standing in front of the sink with her head down, leaning on her hands when Faulkner returned.

He stood behind her and rested his hands next to hers on the counter. Cheyenne could feel his heat along her back. His body was one big muscle and she loved how he felt against her. She felt safe and cared for. It was crazy, but it was also a feeling she knew she couldn't get accustomed to. She should be more freaked that this man, this stranger, had apparently spent the night in her apartment, and was still there, but she couldn't muster up the outrage. He'd done nothing but take care of her. Cheyenne knew she could trust him, but she wasn't sure why he'd spent the night.

"Why are you here?" Cheyenne asked seriously, lifting her head to look at Faulkner in the mirror.

"Because you need me."

"But we don't know each other."

"We know each other better than some people do after a couple of dates."

"Yeah, but we haven't even *been* on a date."

"Which is something I mean to remedy soon."

"Do you have a comeback to everything I say?" Cheyenne was frustrated with Faulkner's calm and rational answers to everything she brought up.

"Yes. Now, are you ready for the bandages to come off?"

Cheyenne nodded, then rolled her eyes when Faulkner didn't move, but just raised his eyebrow at her instead. "Yes, I'm ready for the bandages to come off."

Dude merely smiled at her. He stepped back a foot and let her turn in his arms. He reached behind him to pull out a wicked looking knife from somewhere behind him.

"Jesus, Faulkner. Is *that* necessary to carry around?"

He looked down at the k-bar knife in his hand. "Yeah, Shy, it's necessary. I'm just sorry I didn't have it with me yesterday when I was trying to remove all that damn tape from your arms. It was in my truck, but it was a huge fuck up on my part not to have it on me."

Dude wasn't going to say anything else, but the knife had saved his life more than once. He brought it up to her arm and said, "Stay still." He wasn't going to cut her, he'd rather face ten terrorists with no weapon than hurt this woman, but her standing still would certainly help make *sure* he didn't hurt her.

Dude felt Cheyenne go stiff and smothered the smile he could feel forming on his face. He felt lucky as hell she'd been as trusting of him as she had been so far. If she'd told him how she'd woken up and found a man she barely knew in her apartment after a hell of a day, and didn't immediately kick him out, he would've paddled her ass. But since it was him, and since he knew he'd never hurt even one hair on her head, he didn't say a word at her easy capitulation.

He ran the knife up the bandage on her right arm, easily slicing it. Dude put the knife on the counter and took both hands to peel back the white gauze slowly and easily. He winced at the rough looking patches of skin that had been irritated by the removal of the tape.

"They look good," Cheyenne said with satisfaction looking down at her arm that had been uncovered.

"Good?"

"Yeah, you should've seen them yesterday. That stuff they put on my arm is obviously miracle goo!"

They both laughed and Dude grabbed the knife again and made short work of the bandages on Cheyenne's other arm. When those too had been removed, Dude stepped back. "Okay, Shy, I think you're okay to shower. Hop in and get clean. I'll be in the kitchen waiting for you. Take your time."

Cheyenne nodded and watched as Faulkner backed out of the small bathroom and closed the door behind him. She shook her head in bemusement. She'd planned on spending the day loafing around and being lazy. She had no idea what the day held in store for her now. She didn't know why she trusted Faulkner. Maybe it was because she'd seen him in the store before. Maybe it was because he was in the military. Maybe it was because of the extreme situation she'd been in the day before and he'd been gentle, and had saved her life. Whatever it was, Cheyenne knew it was probably stupid, but she couldn't muster up any alarm that he was in her apartment, and had apparently been there all night. Shrugging, she turned toward the shower and turned on the water, letting it get hot as she removed the scrubs she'd slept in.

Cheyenne spent way too long in the shower, but it felt heavenly. She scrubbed her skin as hard as she dared, and could stand. The hot water felt like it washed her worries away along with the dirt and grime from her ordeal the day before.

She finally turned off the water and stepped from the shower stall. Sitting on the counter was a change of clothes that definitely hadn't been there when she started her shower. Cheyenne blushed furiously, knowing Faulkner had been in the room while she'd been completely naked just a few steps away. Had he seen anything? Did he like what he might have seen?

Cheyenne had been honest with him in that she didn't think she was horrible looking. She did like parts of her body, but others she could take or leave. Cheyenne wasn't huge, she wasn't skinny. She didn't have long hair, she didn't have short hair. She didn't have lavender or ice blue eyes, she had normal brown eyes. She wasn't short, but she wasn't tall either. She was right smack in the middle of everything. Pretty darn normal. Her mom and sister had told her often enough that she was nothing special, and while Cheyenne knew she shouldn't listen to what they said, in this case they were more right than wrong.

Cheyenne quickly dressed in the clothes he'd left on the counter, blushing at Faulkner's choice of underwear. It was obvious he'd had to dig deep in her undie drawer to find the black lace nylon thong. She normally didn't wear such a thing, and she knew it'd been buried under the more practical cotton and nylon bikini underwear. She wasn't going to put them on, but she couldn't resist. She felt tingly and beautiful knowing Faulkner had picked it out and she was now wearing it.

He'd also pulled out a pair of gray sweat bottoms and a V-neck shirt which plunged way too deep for Cheyenne's peace of mind. The bra he'd also dug out of her drawer was the one push up bra she owned. She'd bought it on a whim, thinking it might make her feel sexy, but it hadn't, it'd made her feel uncomfortable and like she was falsely advertising something she didn't have. But now, wearing it because Faulkner had picked it out? She got it. She felt sexy.

Cheyenne looked at herself in the mirror when she'd finished dressing. The bra made her have more cleavage than ever before, and it definitely lived up to its name. It pushed her boobs up and accented them inside the low cut shirt. Cheyenne knew she should probably put on a regular T-shirt, and probably one of her regular bras, but she made herself walk out of the door of the bathroom and into her room.

She might never have a chance like this again. She had no idea where this, whatever this was, was going to go, maybe nowhere, but she'd ride the wave for as long as she could. She'd be a fool not to. She had no idea what Faulkner was still doing there. Cheyenne had been honest, too honest, thanks to the pain killers, last night when she'd questioned what Faulkner was doing with her, but it was no more clear now in the morning when her mind wasn't clouded by drugs as it was last night.

Cheyenne walked into the main area of her apartment, and stopped abruptly and stared. Faulkner was standing in her kitchen at the stove holding a spatula over a steaming pan that held what looked like an omelet. He looked up when she entered the room as if he could sense her there.

"Hey, you look a lot better."

His words were innocuous, but the look in his eye was anything but. Cheyenne watched as his eyes went from her feet, up her legs, stopping at her chest for a moment, then coming back up to meet her eyes.

"Thanks."

They looked at each other a beat longer than was truly comfortable, or polite, before Dude looked back down at the omelet he was making. He took a deep breath and tried not to imagine how the underwear he'd picked out would look on her without the sweats and shirt in the way.

He'd opened her drawers looking for something for Cheyenne to wear after her shower and came face to face with her underwear. It was stuffed into a drawer haphazardly, with no organization and nothing was folded.

Dude had been stunned for a moment, then, as if he was watching from far away, saw himself shifting through the cotton until he'd seen the miniscule little black thong on the bottom of the pile of material. He'd plucked it out without thinking and rubbed his thumb over it.

The same thing had happened when Dude had found her bras. They'd all been sensible and comfortable, except for the black lace number with the strategic padding. Dude wasn't an expert, but he knew what the extra material in the corner of the cups was for.

Sneaking another look up at Cheyenne, Dude knew she'd at least put on the bra he'd picked out. He could see more than a hint of her cleavage as she pulled herself up on the stool at the bar that ran along the edge of the kitchen. He smirked as a slight blush came over her face. She'd caught him looking.

Dude turned and grabbed one of the plates he'd placed next to the stove and expertly scooped up the omelet and transferred it to the plate. He took a fork, placed it on the plate and brought it over to Cheyenne.

"You didn't have to cook," Cheyenne tried to protest.

"I know. Eat."

"I didn't have anything in my fridge but salad dressing...You said someone named Fiona brought all of this?"

"Eat, Shy."

Dude smiled as Cheyenne dutifully picked up the fork and cut into the omelet. He didn't move from her side until she'd taken a bite and closed her eyes in enjoyment. He went back to the stove and broke more eggs into the still hot pan. Dude divided his attention between Cheyenne eating and his own omelet.

By the time he finished making his own breakfast, Cheyenne was eating her last bites. She suddenly looked at him in embarrassment. "I'm sorry, I should've waited for you. Jesus, I'm horrible."

"It's fine, Shy. If you'd waited, yours would've been cold."

"But…"

"I said it's fine." Dude knew he was being a bit harsher than the situation called for, but he couldn't help it. It was a part of who he was. He was used to being obeyed. It came from being a SEAL and being in situations where obeying was second nature and necessary for survival. He wasn't into total control and the bullshit that went along with the BDSM lifestyle, but he certainly needed to be in control when he went to bed with a woman.

Dude hadn't really thought about what that might mean in a real relationship, because he'd had never *had* a real relationship. As most of his buddies had done before they'd settled down, he enjoyed picking up women. He'd take them home and have an excellent time for the night. But after that one night, they were gone. Every woman had known the score and none had any complaints, at least none they'd verbalized to him. They'd all willingly turned over control to him and left the next morning, but Dude had never really thought about how it would work for more than a night.

He shook his head. Dude wanted Cheyenne, and not like he'd had other women. He *liked* her. As he'd told her the night before, she was interesting and fun. Those weren't adjectives he'd used to describe women in the past that he'd liked. Hell, he hadn't even bothered to get to know any of the women he'd taken to bed before. That probably made him a dick, but he couldn't change his past now.

Liking a woman and wanting to get to know her before sleeping with her, was new for Dude. He'd also never invited his friends into any relationship, whatever kind of relationship he had with Cheyenne, before. He'd *never* gone out of his way to have a one-night-stand interact with his friends. But here he was, one day after meeting Cheyenne, and he'd voluntarily reached out to his friends for her help. Fiona had been overjoyed to help him out and go shopping for food. Dude hadn't wanted to leave Cheyenne while she was hurt and loopy from whatever drugs the staff at the hospital had given her, so he'd called Cookie, but gotten Fiona instead.

She'd bought enough food for at least a month.

Dude had spent the night on Cheyenne's couch, waking up at least once an hour so he could pop his head into her room and check on her. She'd been dead to the world. She hadn't even stirred when he'd stood by her bedside. And the one time Dude had actually touched Cheyenne, she'd groaned and rolled *toward* him, not away from him. It had been harder than Dude had thought to leave her room after that.

Now here he was, bossing Cheyenne around and generally pushing himself on her. Dude knew he should leave and give her some room, but he honestly didn't want to.

"What were your plans for the day, Shy?"

Cheyenne looked over at Faulkner as he ate. She pushed her plate away and leaned on her elbows. "I hadn't really thought much about it. I usually just hang out on my days off."

"Hell, I didn't even ask what you do for a living. I'm sorry."

Cheyenne shrugged. "It's okay. It's not like we've really had a chance to chat about our lives. Besides, it's not that interesting really. I answer the phone when people call 911."

Dude lowered the forkful of omelet he'd been about to put in his mouth and looked at Cheyenne incredulously. "What?"

Feeling nervous and not knowing why Faulkner was being weird, Cheyenne repeated, "I'm a 911 operator."

"So you help save people's lives when they're in desperate need of someone to help them."

It wasn't a question, but Cheyenne treated it as if it was. "Well, I guess, yeah, but it's actually boring a lot of the time and we get a lot of calls that aren't emergencies we have to deal with."

"Don't downplay it, Shy," Dude scolded. "You help people through some of the worst times in their lives. You're there for them when they reach out. That's amazing."

Feeling uncomfortable with his praise, Cheyenne just shrugged.

Dude tilted his head and looked closer at her. He'd been amazed at her occupation. It wasn't as if he couldn't imagine her doing it. She'd stayed calm the day before in the face of her own mortality, and now he knew why. She had a lot of practice dealing with her emotions in extreme situations. "How do you deal with the stress of the job?"

"What?" Cheyenne was startled by Faulkner's question.

"I said, how do you deal with the stress of your job?"

"Uh, I read? I hang out here at home?"

Faulkner looked at her closely. Cheyenne hadn't answered his question, she'd pretty much answered in the form of a question. "You don't deal with it, do you?"

"It's not a big deal."

"It *is* a big deal, Shy. Hell, even me and my buddies know we have to let off steam after a mission. You have to let it go somehow."

"I know you work with explosives, but what do *you* do, Faulkner?" Cheyenne asked defensively. She wanted to get the attention off of her and since he brought it up, she'd go with it.

"I'm a SEAL."

Cheyenne looked at him in horror. Oh fucking hell.

"No, just no, this isn't right."

Dude put his plate away from himself and leaned into Cheyenne. He didn't like her tone of voice. "What do you mean it isn't right? What I feel about you is as right as I've felt in a long time, Shy."

"I mean, you really *are* a hero. What the *hell* are you doing here?"

Dude stood up and crowded Cheyenne until she leaned back against the bar counter. He put his hands on the counter behind her so he was hovering over her and she couldn't possibly ignore him and what he wanted to say.

"As far as I'm concerned, *you're* the hero, Shy." Dude ignored Cheyenne as she shook her head in denial and continued. "You help people every day. Every damn day. You're their lifeline when they need it. They reach out and you're there."

"But I don't save them. Most of the time they're already dead or dying, or at least someone they know is."

"Shy, Jesus." Dude watched as Cheyenne began to shake.

"No really, most of the time I have no idea what happened, what the outcome is, but I watch the news. Sometimes I see. All I do is call the cops and the paramedics, Faulkner. I call people like *you* to come and do the real saving."

Dude felt sick inside. He didn't like to hear Cheyenne feeling this way about herself, about her job. "Shy, I have a story to tell you. Will you listen with an open mind and really hear what I'm about to tell you?"

At Cheyenne's nod, he simply raised his eyebrows at her.

"Sorry, yes, I'll listen."

"I'm a disappointment to my parents." Dude could tell Cheyenne was about to protest, and he cut her off. "I'm not telling you this to make you feel sorry for me or anything. Just listen."

Cheyenne nodded and watched as a muscle ticked in Faulkner's jaw. Whatever he wanted to tell her was serious.

"I skipped school one day when I was about thirteen. I came home from surfing, expecting to get shit from my parents for skipping, and saw blood all over our kitchen. My parents weren't there. There was no note or anything. I had no idea where they were or what had happened. All I knew was that the house was empty and there was a shitload of blood on the counter, sink, and even on the floor of our kitchen. I completely freaked out. I dialed 911 and was hysterical. The lady who answered the phone was an angel. She got me calmed down and asked me to answer some simple questions. She used a technique I've since heard will engage the right side of the brain and make people think less with their emotional side, and more with the rational side of their brain. She asked what my name was, she asked how old I was, and she asked what my address was. I'm sure you use these techniques too, but by the time she got to the next question I was able to think a bit more clearly.

"I looked around and saw a butcher knife resting next to the cutting board along with a slew of vegetables. While I described what I was seeing, the 911 lady had been doing some investigating of her own. She told me that my mother had been signed into the emergency room by my father. She'd cut herself badly while making dinner and had bled all over the place while she'd waited on my father to help her wrap it up and put pressure on it."

Dude smiled as Cheyenne put one hand on his

bicep and stroked him. She was still looking up at him, brow furrowed, and chewing one lip. Unconsciously, she was trying to soothe him. Dude liked that.

He quickly went to finish his story and make his point. "I was embarrassed as all hell that I'd jumped to conclusions and thought my parents had been stabbed and kidnapped. I never forgot the feeling of relief I had when that lady answered the phone. She was my lifeline, and I don't know what I would've done if she hadn't been there for me. *You* do that for people Shy. You're a lifeline for every person having a crisis that calls and you pick up the phone. I don't know that lady's name, I never met her and never had a chance to thank her properly. I regret that to this day. I wish you could meet every single person you help, Shy. I wish you could see first-hand how much you help them."

Dude paused and brought his scarred hand to the back of Cheyenne's neck. He tilted it up to his and forced her to look into his eyes. "What you do is important, Shy. You touch more lives than you'll ever know. The people you talk to will never forget you and what you do for them, even if their loved one doesn't survive. Own it, hon. Be proud of yourself."

Cheyenne closed her eyes briefly, loving the feel of Faulkner's thumb at her chin and his pinky on the back of her neck. It felt awesome. "I'll try," she whispered.

"You do that." Dude got closer into Cheyenne's

space and brought his other hand up from the counter to her side. He stroked his thumb against her waist. "I'm going to kiss the hell out of you, Shy. Then I'll probably touch you way too intimately for having just met you yesterday. I can't stop thinking about you wearing the thong I picked out for you and having it snug against your core as we sit here. Once I force myself to pull away from you, hopefully before I go too far, I'm going to get out of your hair for a few hours. I have some things I have to do, but I'll be back later. I'm going to take you to meet the most important people in my life...my SEAL team and their women. Then I'll take you back to my place and you'll spend the night in my bed while I sleep on the couch. When I finally take you, I want to make sure we're both ready for it. Do you have a problem with any of that?"

Cheyenne tried not to hyperventilate. There were so many things wrong with what Faulkner said, but she wanted every single thing with a desire that boarded on desperation. "I have to work tomorrow," she managed breathlessly.

She watched as Faulkner smiled widely and a bit wickedly. "Okay, I'll bring you back here before your shift so you can change and do whatever it is you have to do to get ready. Will that work? Any other objections?"

Cheyenne went to shake her head, caught herself

and said instead, "No, Faulkner, no objections."

The look in his eyes was electric. "You expressed a thought last night, and you should know that I can't wait to show you how my hand feels against your…skin, Shy." Dude lowered his head, not giving her a chance to respond to his words, and proceeded to kiss the hell out of her as he promised.

He didn't ask, he didn't ease into the kiss, he dove in and took over. Dude didn't give her a chance to take control. He thrust his tongue into Cheyenne's mouth and aggressively took her. He used his teeth, tongue, and even his lips. He teased, nibbled, bit, and stroked her. Within moments, Cheyenne was twisting and turning in his grip, lost in the passion they were sharing.

Dude grabbed hold of her wrists with his right hand and brought them behind her. He held them at the small of her back, encouraging her to arch into him. Dude took his left hand and brushed his knuckles against her breasts, now even more prominently displayed in her low cut shirt and the push up bra.

Dude eased away from Cheyenne's mouth, ignoring her whimper of protest and looked down at his hand caressing her chest. He could see her nipples poking through both the lacy bra and the cotton of the T-shirt.

"Normal? Jesus, Shy, look at you. You are *anything* but fucking *normal*."

Without giving her a chance to say or do anything

else, Dude dropped his head and licked a line between her breasts. He held her still with one hand still clutching her wrists behind her back and the other rested just under her breasts. He could feel her heart hammering against her chest as if she'd run a marathon.

"Beautiful. So beautiful," Dude murmured, pulling back once more. He looked up into Cheyenne's eyes again. "You have no idea how badly I want to take you to the ground, strip off all your clothes and spend the rest of the day tasting you and discovering just how good you feel under me. No fucking clue. This is *not* a one night stand, Shy. Say it."

"Not a one night stand."

"Good. Yeah, no way one night would be enough." Dude struggled with himself. Cheyenne was so beautiful, helpless in his arms, waiting for whatever he was going to do with her next. He knew he was treading on thin ice. He was testing his control to the limit, but he had to taste her.

"Hang on, Shy. I have to feel your nipple on my tongue just once before I let you go." Dude leaned back and took his mangled left hand and stretched the V-neck of her shirt to one side. He was probably ruining it, but he didn't fucking care. He moved it over enough until he could see the edge of the lace on the cup of her bra. Holding her shirt, he used one of the stubs of his fingers to move it out of the way. It only took an inch and her nipple popped out of the cup of her bra and Dude could see it harden further as the cold air of the room hit it.

Cheyenne had large areolas and her nipple was a shade darker than the skin around it. Dude took the nail of his thumb and flicked it over her nipple. He watched as Cheyenne groaned and arched into his touch, pushing herself closer to him. "Fuck. Beautiful." Dude leaned down and sucked Cheyenne into his mouth hard. Just as he'd done with the kiss, he didn't start out slow. He sucked hard and used his teeth to pull on her nipple and elongate it further. Dude felt her arms jerk against his hold as she squirmed against him.

He let go of her nipple with a pop and looked down. If they hadn't been wearing clothes, Dude knew he would've been inside her. They were pressed together intimately and he could swear he could feel Cheyenne's heat through both their clothes.

As his thumbnail continued to flick over her nipple, Dude leaned in and whispered in her ear, "Oh yeah, that thong is soaked, isn't it, Shy? I'd love to brush it up against my cheek now that you've been wearing it. I imagined what it'd feel like, what it'd smell like as I pulled it out of your drawer, but I'll kill to have my hands on it now." Dude heard Cheyenne whimper, and she tilted her neck to the side, inviting him to play.

He sucked her earlobe into his mouth and bit down.

Then Dude moved to her neck. Not caring, he began marking her where everyone would be able to see it. Purposely choosing a place where his mark couldn't be hidden, he sucked Cheyenne's skin into his mouth.

"Are y-y-you giving me a hickey?" Cheyenne stuttered, not fighting him, but tilting her head giving Dude more room to work. "What are we, fifteen?"

Waiting until he'd sufficiently bruised her neck with his mouth, Dude finally lifted his head to check his handiwork. "Hell yeah I'm marking you. I want you to think about my mouth on you, my fingers on your nipple, and your legs squeezing me tight every time you look in the mirror, Shy."

Watching as his fingers plucked at her erect nipple Dude repeated, enunciating each word clearly, "This is not a one night stand. I don't think I'll get ever get enough of you."

Finally, with regret, Dude knew he had to stop or else he *wouldn't* stop. He leaned down and gave her nipple one last long lick, loving how hard she was for him. He licked his way over to her cleavage and tasted her between her breasts one more time. He reluctantly tweaked her nipple one last time with his thumbnail and eased the cup of her bra back over so it covered her breast once more. He leaned in and took her mouth with his again. His left hand shifted so it was up at the back of her neck.

Dude eased back so the only places they were touching were his hand holding her wrists at the small of her back and his other hand on her neck. He waited patiently, with a wide smile on his face, for Cheyenne to open her eyes.

When she finally pried her eyelids up, he was right there, watching as she blushed a fiery red. "You're delicious, Shy. I'm sorry you were caught up in that situation yesterday, but I'm not sorry we met. If that was the only way you could come into my life, then I'm glad you were there. I'm a selfish asshole, but that's how I feel."

Dude waited, when Cheyenne didn't say anything, but continued to look up at him calmly, he continued. "I like you, Cheyenne. I think you're amazing. I'm a demanding son of a bitch in the bedroom, but if this interlude was any indication, we're going to get along just fine."

Cheyenne struggled for the first time, realizing just how much Faulkner had bossed her around. When he didn't let go of her she belatedly glared at him. Her glare obviously had no effect, because he just laughed and held on to her wrists tighter.

"I loved feeling you next to me. I loved feeling you flex against me. If at any time you honestly don't like what we're doing, just tell me. I swear I'll hear you, Shy. Okay?"

"Okay," Cheyenne agreed immediately. Faulkner

hadn't done anything she didn't like so far. It might not be very women's lib of her, but she loved not having to think about anything but enjoying the feelings Faulkner was invoking in her body. She liked that he took charge of their lovemaking.

Dude finally let go of her hands and took a step back from her. He looked down at her in appreciation as she shifted, trying to regain her equilibrium. He ran his index finger down the stretched out V of her shirt, and dipped low between her breasts. Finally he shut his eyes and sighed.

"Okay, now that you think I'm a sex fiend, I'm leaving. I have some stuff to do related to yesterday. I have to debrief my commander and check in again with the police. I'll be back around three to pick you up. We'll be heading to Wolf and Ice's house. They're having an impromptu picnic today.

"Impromptu?"

Dude smiled. "Yeah, as soon as Fiona dropped off the food last night, she called her girl posse and they arranged this get together today so they could meet you." At the startled look in Cheyenne's eyes, Dude leaned in and rested his forehead against hers. "They'll love you, Shy. Trust me. Remember when you said this wasn't a one night stand? This is what I mean. I would never bring a one night stand over to my friend's house to meet my team and their women."

"You made me say that."

"I didn't make you say anything. You said it of your own volition."

"But…"

"No, no buts," Dude cut her off. "This. Is. Not. A. One. Night. Stand." He enunciated quietly and firmly.

Cheyenne smiled. "Okay, Faulkner, whatever you say."

Dude just shook his head at her. She was so damn sweet. His smile dimmed and he looked at Cheyenne seriously. "You all right with this. With us?"

"We just met. It's fast."

"It is. But it feels right. Yes?"

"Yeah."

"Okay then, I'll pick you up at three."

"Okay, Faulkner. I'll be ready."

Dude stepped completely away from Cheyenne. As he backed away from her, he didn't take his eyes off hers until he got to the front door. "Rest today, Shy. Take it easy, don't overdo it. I'll see you later." Then he turned and opened her door. Right before leaving, Dude turned back to Cheyenne. "Lock this behind me." He waited for her to nod, then he disappeared out the door.

Cheyenne padded over to her front door. She dutifully turned the dead bolt and put on the emergency chain, then sagged against the door.

Holy hell, was all she could think to herself as she closed her eyes and smiled.

Chapter Six

CHEYENNE FIDGETED NERVOUSLY as she sat in the truck seat next to Faulkner. He'd come back to her apartment later that afternoon just as he said he would. Cheyenne had spent the day freaking out about what she was supposed to wear to this "get-together" with his friends, what he was really doing with her, why she was even letting him come back and get her…and any other little thing that came to her mind.

This wasn't her. First of all she wasn't the type of woman to move so quickly with a man. Hell, the last man she'd dated, they'd dated for a month before he'd gotten to second base. Secondly, she wasn't the kind of woman men fell for, but God, it felt nice. She'd day-dreamed about Faulkner. Ever since she'd seen him in the grocery store, innocently shopping for food, she'd dreamed he'd take one look at her and declare his undying love. It was stupid, but as her family was constantly telling her, she had her head in the clouds.

Cheyenne had spent the day, between freak outs,

cleaning her apartment from top to bottom. She could admit she was lazy, but knowing Faulkner had been in her craptastic apartment all night, looking at her sloppiness, was too much.

So she cleaned. Cheyenne washed all the dirty dishes that were sitting in the sink, vacuumed, picked up all the junk mail she usually just threw on the coffee table and sorted through it. She wrote out a couple of checks for bills that were due soon and she did a few loads of laundry.

Looking around, Cheyenne figured she probably should dust, but that was going just a bit too far. She never understood dusting. What was the point? It wasn't as if dusting a piece of furniture would make the dust in the air disappear. As soon as she finished wiping down the bookshelf, or table or whatever, the dust in the air would settle right back down…so it was really just a waste of time. Cheyenne also didn't figure Faulkner would even see or care about some dust.

Finally in the early afternoon, Cheyenne knew it was time to see about figuring out what she was going to wear. Cheyenne left on the thong undies with a secret smile. Over the course of the day she'd gotten used to them, and if she was honest with herself, she wanted to please Faulkner by keeping them on.

After trying on, and dismissing, what seemed to be half her wardrobe, Cheyenne settled on a pair of low rider jeans, which weren't too low, she wasn't eighteen years old anymore, a black knit sweater that had a scoop neck in front that showed a hint of cleavage, but not enough to be slutty. Cheyenne did consider for about four point two seconds wearing the push-up bra she'd had on before, but decided against it. Yes, Faulkner had picked it out for her to wear earlier, but it seemed too weird to wear it when she was going to meet his friends.

There was nothing she could do about the bruise Faulkner had left on the side of her neck, but if she was being honest with herself, it made her smile every time she looked at it. She'd only had a hickey once before in her life, back in junior high school. The boy who'd given it to her had sucked way too hard on her and the bruise that had resulted was horrific. She'd worn a turtle neck for at least a week until it had healed enough not to be gruesome looking. But Faulkner's mark, was subtle. He'd applied just the right of pressure to mark her, but not to make her look like she was thirteen and experimenting with sex.

Her shirt had long sleeves to cover her still-healing arms, which was one of the most important check boxes for Cheyenne for the night. She didn't want to stand out too much when she met Faulkner's friends, and if she wore a short sleeve shirt, she certainly would. She put on a pair of black flip flops with sparkly rhinestones along the material on the top, and finished off the outfit with a pair of dangly fake diamond earrings.

Cheyenne couldn't really do anything about her black eye though. She'd never really learned how to put on make-up and figured if she tried now she'd look like a teenage girl playing with her mom's make-up kit for the first time. She swiped some mascara over her lashes and put on some peppermint flavored lip balm. She stuck the tube in her pocket for reapplication later. She never wore lipstick, but was addicted to flavored lip balm.

Cheyenne figured she looked passable. She'd never win any beauty pageants, but she thought she looked pretty good. The shirt was one of her favorites and the jeans looked good on her. The thirty minutes before Faulkner arrived at her apartment Cheyenne spent pacing the small living room and biting her thumbnail. It was a nasty habit that she'd mostly broken, in part because her sister had teased her unmercifully about it, but she couldn't seem to make herself stop doing it when she was stressed out.

She'd also packed a small overnight bag. Faulkner had informed, not asked, her that she'd be spending the night at his place that night. She wasn't sure if he really meant it, but if he did, she wanted to be ready. Cheyenne knew it was a little weird, and way fast, but what the hell. She decided to live in the moment. Faulkner said, and had made her agree, that whatever was going on with them wasn't a one night stand, but she wasn't sure she truly believed him. She'd go with it though. If all this turned out to be *was* a one night stand, she wasn't going to complain about it. Cheyenne had obsessed about the military guy in the grocery store long enough that there was no way she could, or would, turn him down now. Hell, people had one night stands all the time. She decided to live a little and worry about it all later.

Cheyenne packed a T-shirt and pair of stretchy boy-shorts to sleep in, as well as a casual outfit to change into the next day, another pair of jeans and a V-neck T-shirt this time. Faulkner said he'd bring her home before her shift tomorrow, so she could change into her work clothes then. Cheyenne threw in the things she needed for the morning–shampoo, toothpaste, things like that, and she was done.

Finally when Cheyenne thought she was going to have a heart attack, Faulkner was there. She opened the door and watched as his eyes did a full body sweep. When his eyes finally met hers, it was obvious he liked what he saw.

"Maybe we can stay in instead."

Huh?

"What?"

Dude shook his head as if to clear it. "Fuck. No, we have to go, everyone is waiting for us."

"You don't want to go anymore?" Cheyenne's thumb came up to her mouth unconsciously. If Faulkner had taken one look at her and decided he didn't want to take her to meet his friends anymore, she was going to die.

Dude saw the look of uncertainty in Cheyenne's eyes and mentally kicked himself. He took a step forward until he was in her space. Satisfaction ran through him when she didn't step out of his way.

He put his right hand on her arm and brought his scarred left hand up to her face. In the past he never would've even thought about touching a woman with his mangled hand, but Cheyenne didn't seem to mind it in the least. In fact, if her words and actions in the car the night before were any indication, she enjoyed it.

"Shy, I want you to meet my friends more than anything. They're going to love you, you're going to love them. But the second I saw you, the only thing I could think about was how you'd look lying on your bed, looking up at me the same way you did when I opened the door. I'm trying to go slowly here, to prove to you, and me, that this isn't a one-time thing. I've never had to hold myself back before, so I'm learning as I go. The words popped out of my mouth before I could stop them."

Cheyenne was looking up at him with wide eyes. Faulkner could see her nipples peak through the knit shirt she was wearing. He shut his eyes for a moment then opened them again and willed her to understand.

"I say what I mean, Shy. If I didn't want you to meet my friends, you wouldn't. If I wanted to be your friend, and only your friend, you'd know. I'm a simple man. If I'm tired, I sleep, if I'm hungry, I eat. But know this...I want you. I want nothing more than to take you into your bedroom and watch as you take your clothes off for me. I want you to watch me, just as you are right now, as I strip for you. I want to take you hard and fast, then I want it slow and sweet. I want you in your shower and on every piece of furniture in my house. I want to take you from behind as your hands are tied together behind your back, and I want to watch as you take me down your throat until I explode. All these thoughts ran through my mind in the split second after you opened the door and I saw you. That's why I said what I did, not because I don't want you to meet my friends. Got it? Don't doubt me, Shy."

Cheyenne could only look up at Faulkner. Her brain was officially fried. She could feel how slick she'd gotten with his words and she knew if she looked down she'd be embarrassed at how tight her nipples had gotten with his words.

"I got it. You certainly put any fears I had to rest about whether or not you wanted me to meet your friends."

"Good. One more thing."

"Yeah?"

"You're not wearing the bra I pulled out earlier. Why?"

Cheyenne blushed, she wasn't sure Faulkner would've noticed. "You can tell?"

Dude loved the rosy hue that bloomed over Cheyenne's face and neck. He'd wanted to pull her into his arms and cart her off to her bedroom more than he wanted to breathe, but he controlled himself...barely. "Yeah, I can tell. You've got beautiful tits, Shy. They don't sag and sit high on your chest. But when you were wearing that bra earlier, they were pushed up even higher, and the cleavage it created made me want to bury my face between your flesh and spend hours worshiping you there. So yeah, I can tell."

Dude brought his right hand up to her chest and caressed the top of her breasts that were showing above the scoop neck of her shirt.

"I...uh...Do I look okay in this sweater without it?"

Dude didn't like the uncertainty in Cheyenne's words. Damn. He mentally kicked himself again. He was saying all the wrong things tonight. He knew Cheyenne wasn't confident in herself and how she looked. He'd have to work on that.

"I think I already covered how 'okay' you look in that shirt, Shy. And on second thought, my teammates might be married, but I don't want them ogling you all night, and ogle they would do if you were wearing that bra. I think I'll have to make sure you only wear your sexy lingerie when we're alone." Dude watched as Cheyenne gave him a small shy smile.

Dude pulled Cheyenne forward, put his right hand under her chin and lifted her head so he could get at her with the perfect angle, and kissed her long and deep. The kiss was over way too quickly, but Dude knew he had to get them out of there. Every word he'd spoken was the God's honest truth, and if he didn't get them gone, they wouldn't go.

Dude pulled back. "Peppermint. Every time I kiss you, you taste different."

"It's my lip balm," Cheyenne told him softly.

"I love it." Dude left his right hand under her chin, forcing her to look at him, and took his left hand and curled his remaining fingers down and ran the stubs of his fingers over the mark on the side of her neck, her collarbone, then down over the swells of her breasts. Without looking away from her eyes, Dude moved his hand lower and ran his hand over the nipple on her right breast. Feeling it peak even more than it was before, he finally looked down.

"Damn, Shy, You're so fucking responsive."

"I haven't been before," Cheyenne said the words without thought, then cringed. Shit.

Not freaking out over her mention of being with other men, Dude commented, "Oh man, we're going to have fun aren't we?" Taking a deep breath, Dude moved his hand so it gently grasped her arm. "Did you pack a bag? You're coming to my place tonight."

Cheyenne nodded shyly at him, and pointed to her bag sitting next to the door.

Dude took a deep breath, the sight of her pre-packed bag, knowing she'd done what he'd asked of her without balking, did something to him. Yes, he'd told her to, but ultimately she made the decision to do it. It was what he loved best about being with submissive women. They held all the power. He could order Cheyenne around all he wanted, but in the end, she was the one who allowed it or not. Dude leaned down and grabbed the small bag, suddenly wishing it had a lot more in it, and said, "Come on, we have to go. Now."

Cheyenne smiled at him. Faulkner liked to boss her around, it was obvious he liked to be in control in the bedroom, but she could still get to him. She liked that.

Now they were sitting in his truck on the way to Ice and Wolf's house.

"Tell me about your friends again?" Cheyenne asked as they headed down the road.

"Wolf is the team leader. Ice is his woman and she's a chemist. She saved his life when they were on a plane that was hijacked."

"I remember that! Holy shit! That was *your* SEAL team?" Fascinated by the blush that stole over Faulkner's face, Cheyenne waited for him to continue.

"Yeah, that was us. They went through a whole bunch of shit, but eventually Caroline moved out here to be with him. They recently got married. Then there's Abe and Alabama. Things were great with them until Abe said some shit after Alabama got arrested and he fought like hell to get her back. I don't think I've ever seen a couple more in love and connected at the hip than those two. As SEALs, we're born and bred to protect others, but Abe certainly fucked up by not protecting Alabama's emotions. Thank God she forgave him.

"Cookie and Fiona were the next to get together. Fiona was kidnapped by a sex slave ring and taken over the border. Cookie was the one to go in and find her and bring her out. Mozart and Summer are the most recent of us to get together. Mozart had been hunting the man who killed his little sister when he was a teenager and somehow the man found out about Summer and wanted to torture Mozart by taking his woman. Benny and I are the last ones of our team without women."

Silence filled the cab of the truck when Dude had finished speaking. He turned to look at Cheyenne. She was staring at him incredulously.

Dude chuckled. "Yeah, it sounds crazy, but I swear they're all normal people and they're gonna love you."

"Maybe we should go back." Cheyenne was freaking out. A chemist? Sex slave ring? Arrested? Kidnapping? She was in way over her head.

"Nope. You don't see it do you?"

"See what?"

"Think about how *we* met, Shy."

"Oh hell."

"Exactly. Now when people talk about us they'll talk about how I saved your life when you had a bomb strapped to your chest. That's just as dramatic as the way my friends met their women. Relax, Cheyenne." Dude turned to her as they stopped at a red light and put his hand on her knee. "I would never put you in a position where you'd feel unwelcome. You might be a little uncomfortable at first, it's hard to meet new people, but I know by the end of the night you'll have four new girlfriends and you'll have the respect of the guys on my team. Just relax."

Chewing on her nail, Cheyenne said, "Okay, I'll try."

Dude pulled her thumb out of her mouth and pulled it to his own lips and sucked on it for a moment before letting go. He laughed at the wide eyed look Cheyenne was giving him.

"Don't chew on your nail. Anytime I see you doing

it, I'm going to do that same thing. I don't care where we are. Keep that in mind."

"Uh…"

Dude just laughed and patted her on her knee as he turned his attention back to the traffic.

Deciding to be amused, rather than pissed, Cheyenne finally laughed at him. "I'm not sure that's really a deterrent, Faulkner."

He just grinned at her. "Oh, I think you'll find it is if you don't want to find your nipples hard as rocks and squirming in your seat in front of others. I bet I could have you doing both just by sucking on that thumb." Dude laughed as he watched Cheyenne shift in her seat.

He didn't filter the words that came to his mind, just shot them out there. "Jesus, Shy, if my words can do that to you, you're going to love what my mouth can do."

"Stop, Faulkner. Seriously. I don't…I can't…"

Dude sobered quickly at seeing her unease. "I'm sorry, Shy. I'll tone it down. I keep forgetting how new this is to you and that you aren't used to it."

"I just…Fuck. Why can't I talk around you?"

"You could talk last night," Dude reminded her.

"Yeah, that's because the evil doctors drugged me up. I didn't know taking hard core prescription drugs loosened my tongue like that."

The car stopped in front of a small house in a cute

111

SUSAN STOKER

neighborhood. There was a small porch and there were various cars and trucks parked in the driveway and along the street. Cheyenne didn't think she was ready for this after all.

"Hey, look at me for a second, Cheyenne."

She turned her head and wiped her hands down her thighs. Cheyenne was feeling more nervous about meeting Faulkner's friends than when she'd been waiting to answer her first emergency call at work.

"If you want to go, we'll go. We don't have to do this now."

That wasn't what Cheyenne thought Faulkner would say. "But you wanted me to meet your friends."

"And I still do, but I don't want you to make yourself sick over it. I rushed this, I know it, I'm sorry. But I like you. And I wanted you to meet the most important people in my life. We'll have plenty of time to do this later. It was a stupid idea."

Cheyenne watched as Faulkner reached for the keys still hanging in the ignition. She put her hand out and placed it on his forearm, stopping him from starting the truck again.

"I'm nervous, I won't deny that, but I want to meet them. I *do*. I don't get out much, Faulkner. It wouldn't matter if I met them today or three months from now, I'd still be nervous, partly because I'm meeting new people, but also because they're so important to *you*. I like you." Cheyenne dropped her eyes and fiddled with a string hanging off of the seat in front of her. "What if they don't like me? What if we have nothing in common? I...I want to get to know you better and knowing how important they are to you, I know we could never last if they didn't like me."

Dude knew this was an important moment and he struggled to find the right words so Cheyenne would understand. "Trust me when I tell you they'll like you, Shy. Alabama was a janitor when she met Abe. She spent her evenings cleaning offices in buildings. Caroline is a chemist, but she'd just lost her parents when she met Wolf. She was on her way across the country to a new job because she had no ties to California. No one reported Fiona missing when she was taken. She didn't have any close friends or family that worried about her. Summer was divorced and was flat broke when she met Mozart and was working as a maid for a dump of a motel. These are not women who'll judge you. I promise. And in case it wasn't already obvious, I like you too. And in the extremely low chance you don't get along with the other women, I'll still want to get to know you better." Dude paused for a moment then said, "It's your choice, Shy. I'd never force you to do anything you didn't want to do. *Anything*."

Cheyenne knew there was more to what he'd said than simply meeting his friends, but she put it aside for the moment.

"Okay, let's go. Shit. I had a damn bomb strapped to my chest, how hard can this be?"

Dude laughed and reached out for Cheyenne. He pulled her to him for a quick hard kiss then let her go. "Wait there, I'll come around."

Cheyenne rolled her eyes, but waited for Faulkner to come around the truck and open her door for her.

He tucked her arm in his and they ambled up the front walk to the house. Cheyenne took a deep breath and steeled herself for whatever was going to happen. She decided right there to do whatever it took to enjoy herself. These people were important to Faulkner, and she wanted them to like her more than was probably healthy. She warned herself not to be a dork, a spaz, or a flake. She'd just be herself. Hopefully that'd be enough.

Chapter Seven

"**F**AULKNER!"

Cheyenne took a step back as the front door burst open and a brunette dynamo slammed into Faulkner. He took a step back and laughed as his arms came around the woman and lifted her off her feet.

"Hey, Alabama. How are you?"

"It's been too long since we've seen you!" Alabama pulled back and kissed Faulkner on the cheek. Suddenly turning and pinning her eyes on Cheyenne, Alabama said, "Oh shit, I'm sorry, it's just been too long since I've seen him. That was so rude of me. Jeez."

Cheyenne relaxed a bit. She immediately liked this woman. "It's okay, really."

Dude leaned down, kissed Alabama on the cheek, then turned to Cheyenne. "Come on, Shy, let's go inside and I'll introduce you to everyone."

Cheyenne nodded and smiled at Alabama as they made their way inside. They went into the living room and Cheyenne froze. Shit. She knew there would be a lot of people there, but seeing them all in the same place at the same time was daunting. Looking around at the muscular men, Cheyenne sighed. She knew it. She leaned into Faulkner and stood on tiptoe. He leaned down toward her so she could reach his ear and she told him earnestly, "I knew it, you *do* hang out with a gang of hotties!"

Dude threw his head back and laughed. God, his Shy was fucking hilarious.

Cheyenne looked at Faulkner with a small smile on her face. She loved when he laughed. She remembered how serious he'd been at the store when he was working on the bomb. Being able to put some levity into his life seemed like the best gift anyone could have given her.

"Girl, you're officially one of us now. I've never seen Faulkner laugh like that before. Ever."

Remembering where they were and who they were standing in front of, Cheyenne blushed and looked at the woman who'd spoken.

"I'm Caroline. It's so good to meet you. When Fiona called and said that Faulkner needed her to get some food over to your apartment, it was all we could do not to all bust over there. We're so glad you came over today. I'm sure you're freaked, we all were when we had to meet each other. Just know you aren't alone."

Cheyenne smiled, liking the other woman immediately. It seemed there was a lot of "saying it like it was" around these people.

"It's good to meet you too, Caroline. Thanks for having me over today."

A big man came over to stand next to Caroline. He looked older than the other men, but he was absolutely gorgeous. He had large muscles that Cheyenne could see rippling under his shirt.

"Let me make the introductions before you have to use mind-melding skills to figure out who everyone is."

Before he could continue, Caroline poked him in the ribs and looked up. "And tell her everyone's real names. You can't just use nicknames."

Wolf smiled indulgently down at Caroline. "Yes, dear."

Caroline rolled her eyes.

Cheyenne smiled again and relaxed a fraction. They all seemed so…normal. Faulkner put his arm around her waist and she turned to him for a moment. He smiled down at her then leaned down. "Told you they'd like you," he whispered.

Cheyenne just shook her head. She'd only been there for like two point three minutes, the jury was still out in her mind, but it did look good…so far.

"I'm Wolf, or Matthew if you prefer, and this is Caroline, my wife. Sometimes you'll hear us call her Ice, that's her nickname."

Cheyenne watched as Matthew looked down at

Caroline with so much love, and lust, it made her blush. She tried to ignore the big man standing next to her, and concentrated on the introductions.

"Over there is Mozart, or Sam, and his woman Summer. Next to them is Cookie, or Hunter, and Fiona. Then there's Abe, whose real name is Christopher, and Alabama. And that lonely looking guy over there is Benny, or Kason. He's the last one of us to find a woman."

"Hey!" Benny protested, "I've got women!"

Everyone laughed.

Cheyenne laughed with everyone else, but inside was quaking. How in the hell would she ever remember who everyone was? She was horrible at names. The first thing she did every time the phone rang at work and she asked the person on the line what their name was, was write it down on a sticky pad next to her keyboard. Shit, she already forgot most of the people's names already, and she was *just* told them all.

"Everyone, this is Cheyenne Cotton. Please don't freak her out tonight. Keep all the scary and weird stories to yourself. I don't want her to run screaming from the house."

Cheyenne waved self-consciously at the group. God, this was awkward.

"Okay then," Caroline said, taking charge of the group. "Matthew, you and Christopher go and grill up the steaks. Anyone want to help me with the rest of the grub?"

Cheyenne immediately spoke up. The last thing she wanted to do was stand around while everyone else got the food ready. "I will."

Caroline smiled at her. "Great. Thanks. I could use the help."

Cheyenne went to follow Caroline into the kitchen, but Faulkner wouldn't let go of her waist. She looked up at him questionably.

He just looked at her intently for a moment.

"What?" Cheyenne whispered, suddenly wondering if she should've offered to help after all.

"Thank you."

"For what?"

"For being here. For helping. For trying, for me."

"They seem very nice, Faulkner. I'm glad you brought me."

Cheyenne could tell there was more Faulkner wanted to say, but instead he leaned down and kissed her on her forehead. He let his lips linger for a beat longer than was probably proper in front of his friends, with a woman he'd met only the day before, but he soon brought his head back up.

"Go make me food, woman."

Cheyenne laughed and smacked him on the arm. "Whatever, *Dude*."

Dude squeezed Cheyenne's waist affectionately and let her go. She headed off to the kitchen smiling.

CHEYENNE LOOKED AROUND the crowded room contentedly. The evening had been wonderful. She'd relaxed much sooner than she'd thought possible. The women were funny and cheerful and didn't care if they said something stupid or silly in front of her or the men.

And the men. Holy smokes. Cheyenne actually pinched herself at one point to make sure it was really real. That she was really sitting in a house with six incredibly hot men chit-chatting. It was surreal.

She hadn't remembered everyone's name, and she certainly didn't know which nickname went with which man, but ultimately it didn't matter. She just went with the flow, and no one seemed to notice.

"I'm stuffed. Jesus, Caroline, did you have to make so much damn food?" Fiona complained. She was sitting in an easy chair on Hunter's lap. Cheyenne could see Hunter's hand absently stroking her hip.

"I might have overdone it a bit, but it was all so good wasn't it?"

"I think if I ate one more bite I would explode like the guy in that Monty Python movie did," Alabama grumbled laughing.

"I loved that movie," Cheyenne spoke up. Parroting

the line from the movie, she said in a fake British accent, "I couldn't eat another bite."

Everyone laughed, and Cheyenne smiled at them all.

"How's school going?" Dude asked Alabama, knowing she was working toward her degree.

"It's good. It's the helicopter parents that are really crazy. There was one mother that actually came to class to take notes for her kid. It was ridiculous. It's hard sometimes to be in classes with teenagers who have no idea what the world is really like though. If they had any idea how precious an education is they'd work harder at it and not take it for granted."

"That is so true," Summer said. "I worked my butt off for my degree and loved every minute of working in Human Resources."

"I remember when I worked at a University in Texas I'd have to deal with those kind of parents every day. I even had a parent call once for her *thirty one* year old son. He couldn't figure out how to order a transcript. It's crazy!" Fiona added, shaking her head.

Cheyenne would've loved to have asked questions, but kept her mouth shut and just let the conversation flow around her. Hopefully in the future she'd get to know these women better and would have a better understanding of what made them tick and she could contribute to the conversation and not feel weird about it.

"Ice, did you ever figure out that new compound you were working on?"

Caroline laughed at Benny's question. "Do you want the technical answer, or the short answer?"

Knowing she could go on all night about chemicals and what she did, Benny smiled and told her, "The short answer."

"Yes."

Everyone laughed when Caroline didn't elaborate.

"Good job then. Congratulations."

"Thanks, Benny. Hopefully in the future it'll mean a lot of people won't have to go through such horrible treatment for some of the worst diseases out there if it does what we think it should."

There was quiet for a moment in the room, then Summer asked, "So what do you do, Cheyenne?"

Cheyenne shifted uncomfortably on the couch. Faulkner was sitting next to her and of course he noticed. "Summer," he warned his friend, knowing Cheyenne was still working through her feelings about her job and hating that Summer had unintentionally put Cheyenne on the spot.

Cheyenne quickly broke in, and put her hand on Faulkner's thigh to ease him. "No, it's okay. It's not a big deal. I answer phones for a living."

"Oh, so you're in customer service or something?"

"Not exactly. I'm an emergency services operator."

No one said anything for a moment, then Fiona asked apologetically, "What does that mean exactly? I'm sorry if I should know, I just don't."

"Oh no, don't feel bad, I should've explained better. I answer the phone when people call in with an emergency. If there's a fire or someone's having a heart attack or something like that."

"You answer 911 calls?" Caroline asked in a weird voice.

Cheyenne looked at Caroline who was sitting across the room in another big fluffy arm chair. She too was sitting in her man's lap, and Cheyenne watched as Matthew's eyes immediately went to his wife. He didn't look happy at the tone of her voice. He looked worried.

Cheyenne tensed. Oh shit. Was Caroline offended? Did she have a bad experience with 911 in the past?

"It's okay, Shy," Dude murmured next to her, sensing her discomfort. He put his arm around her shoulder and pulled her into his side.

"Yeah, I answer 911 calls," Cheyenne told Caroline carefully.

Cheyenne watched as Caroline unfolded herself from Matthew's lap and stood up. Cheyenne risked a glance at the other people in the room. The women's faces were soft, the men's weren't exactly hard, but they weren't relaxed either. Something was happening and Cheyenne had no idea what it was.

Caroline came across the small room to stand in front of Cheyenne. She went to her knees in front of her and put her hands on Cheyenne's knees.

Cheyenne didn't know what to do. She risked a quick glance at Faulkner, but his eyes were locked on Caroline. Cheyenne turned back to the woman kneeling at her feet nervously, not knowing what to expect.

"Thank you. It's obvious you have no idea how important what you do is."

Cheyenne didn't know what to say, so she said nothing.

"I've always wished I could've met the 911 operator that helped me."

Oh shit, Cheyenne didn't know if she was ready to hear this story. She tensed and Faulkner tightened his hold on her and grabbed her left hand with his scarred one. Cheyenne gripped his hand as if it was the only thing standing between her and the firing squad.

Cheyenne heard Faulkner tell Caroline, "I already told her this, Ice, but I'm not sure she really understood. Tell her your story. Maybe between all of us we can convince her how she changes people lives."

"Faulkner…"

"Shhhh, Shy. Listen."

Cheyenne turned back to Caroline, then flicked her eyes up to Matthew. He was looking at Caroline with affection from his seat across the room. He'd sat up and was resting his forearms on his knees. He looked relaxed, but Cheyenne knew he could be across the room in a heartbeat if he needed to be.

"When I lived in Virginia, I was followed home from work one day. Matthew and the rest of the team were away on a mission. I'd just started my job and didn't really know anyone yet. A man broke into my apartment and I had to hide in my shower. I was really scared and called 911 almost without thought. Every kid is taught from a young age to call when they need help, and that's just what I did. I didn't have a long conversation with the lady on the other end of the line, but she was awesome. She didn't panic and had the police on their way within seconds of hearing what my problem was.

"I have no idea who she was or what her name was, but she was my lifeline. I'll never forget her. So on behalf of that lady, and for anyone who has ever called 911, thank you. Thank you for being there. Thank you for caring enough to try to help us. Just thank you."

Cheyenne watched as Caroline's eyes filled with tears and she lay her head down on Cheyenne's knee. Cheyenne lifted a hand and put it on the back of Caroline's head. "I...you're welcome." Cheyenne didn't know what else to say, she was uncomfortable and touched at the same time.

Caroline finally lifted her head and gave Cheyenne a

watery smile. "You, my friend, will have good karma for the rest of your life because of what you do."

Cheyenne was embarrassed and hoped the conversation would soon switch so it wasn't focused on her anymore. She still wasn't ready to jump up and down with glee about her job, but Caroline and Faulkner had started her on the path to thinking that maybe she really did make a difference in the world. At least for some people.

"So…how about them LA Kings huh?" Benny said, trying to lighten the mood of the room, and succeeding.

Everyone laughed. Caroline stood up and wiped the tears from her eyes. She walked back to Matthew and he pulled her into his lap and kissed her deeply.

Cheyenne watched as Matthew put his hand on the back of her head and shifted her until she was lying sideways over his lap. Her legs were dangling over one of the arms of the chair and her upper body was supported by Matthew's arm. Wow.

Cheyenne shifted in her chair and shivered when Faulkner whispered in her ear. "Told you *you* were amazing."

She just smiled.

After a bit more time had passed, Hunter turned on the television. The group was feeling mellow after the large meal, emotional revelations, and spending time with good friends.

After watching a mindless sitcom, the evening news came on. Cheyenne stiffened in surprise when she heard the newscaster say her name. They all watched in fascination as the anchor spoke while a clip from the day before was shown.

"*In other news, Cheyenne Cotton was released from the hospital last night after suffering only superficial wounds in the bomb threat at Kroger yesterday afternoon. Five men were killed after they strapped a bomb to Ms. Cotton and tried to negotiate their way out of the store. A bomb ordinance technician from the Navy was called in to defuse the explosive. Here they are leaving the store after the bomb was neutralized.*"

Cheyenne watched in shock as a video of her and Faulkner coming out of the store was shown. She looked pale and she was holding his hand as he led the way across the broken glass from the front of the store toward the ambulance. She watched as they were surrounded by reporters and Faulkner put his arm around her waist to steady her. The clip ended and the camera panned back to the anchorman sitting behind a desk as he finished his story.

"*The five men who were killed, seemed to be working independently. As of now, the police can't confirm or deny if they were part of a gang. The authorities are withholding their names because of the ongoing investigation. Ms. Cotton has declined any interviews and the Navy isn't releasing the name of the bomb technician that defused the bomb and saved many lives yesterday. We will continue to investigate the story and will report back with any new information. Next up is Tina with the weather for the week..."*

No one said anything for a moment until Mozart breathed, "Jesus, Cheyenne, we had no idea that was *you*. Are you all right? Should you even be out and about?"

Cheyenne couldn't help but giggle. Jesus, these guys were all the same. Protective to the bone. "I'm okay. Faulkner got there in time."

Dude spoke up. "The bastards wrapped her up in so much duct tape it took me ten minutes to get to the damn bomb. The tape ripped off parts of the skin on her arms and you can see the black eye she has from the assholes as well."

Cheyenne glared up at Faulkner. "I can talk, you know."

"I know, but what would come out of your mouth would probably be something like, 'I'm fine, thanks for asking,'" Dude said in a high pitched voice, mocking her.

Cheyenne could hear the other women giggling. She tried to keep her mouth from twitching, but couldn't. It was funny, dammit.

"Well, I *am* all right, Faulkner, and it was nice of them to ask."

That made everyone around the room laugh out

right.

"You guys are hilarious," Fiona told them. "We're so glad Faulkner was there yesterday. Seriously, he's the best at the bomb thing."

"The bomb thing?" Dude mock growled.

"Yeah, the whole bomb thing."

Cheyenne watched as the group bantered back and forth. She'd never had friends like this. Hell, her own family didn't tease each other at all. When Karen picked on her, it had been vicious, and not teasing at all. This was nice. She really liked Faulkner's friends.

Cheyenne didn't realize she was fading until she heard Faulkner say, "It's time for us to go. Shy can't keep her eyes open."

At that Cheyenne forced her eyes to open all the way and watched as Faulkner stood up and shook his friends' hands.

"Yeah, it's time for all of us to get going too. PT is gonna suck in the morning," Mozart groaned.

"You want to use the restroom before you go, Cheyenne?" Caroline asked politely.

"Please."

Cheyenne followed Caroline down a hallway to the small guest bathroom tucked away. Caroline turned to her before she entered.

"I was serious about what I said in there, Cheyenne."

Cheyenne merely nodded. She didn't really want to get into it again. She liked Caroline, but there was only so many "thank you's" she could handle in one night.

"I'm so glad you and Faulkner are together. He deserves someone like you in his life. I'd probably be dead if it wasn't for him and the rest of guys in there."

"I'm not sure we're actually together, Caroline," Cheyenne told her honestly. "I mean, we just met yesterday, under pretty extreme circumstances."

"I know you think that, but you don't really understand these guys. The only time we met any woman of Faulkner's was when we met at *Aces Bar and Grill* or a restaurant. He was never serious about any of them. Ever. He had a wall up. He's a black and white kind of guy. He's either one hundred percent in, or he's not. And believe me, girlfriend, he's one hundred percent into you. As much as I like you, I have to say this. Faulkner is my friend. Don't hurt him. If you aren't into him, leave now. I'll call you a taxi. He'll be pissed, but he'll get over it. If you don't want a long term relationship with him, don't lead him on."

"But…"

"Let me finish. Please."

At Cheyenne's nod, Caroline continued. "These guys fall fast. They're really big teddy bears under all their gruffness. Faulkner wants you. I can see it. We can all see it, but I'm not sure *you* see it. If you just want to sleep with a SEAL, please find someone other than Faulkner."

"Are you kidding?" Cheyenne didn't want to piss Caroline off, but she really couldn't believe the words that were coming out of her mouth.

"No."

"I mean seriously, you think I *wanted* to come over here tonight? Really? When the gorgeous man I've been semi-stalking in the grocery store saves my life and seems to be, by some freaking miracle, interested in me, wants me to come and meet his teammates and friends, do you think I *wanted* to go with him? I knew you guys would judge me. I *knew* it. I don't make friends easily. I didn't know how you guys would take to me. I wanted you to like me and I wanted to like you back, but I thought it was too soon. But I did it. Because I want to be with Faulkner. I'm into him. I'm so into him that if he wanted to tie me to his bed and have his wicked way with me tonight, and every fucking night, I'd do it, without a second thought. I trust him that much."

Not noticing the attention her raised voice was garnering from the group who was now standing at the end of the hall behind her, gaping at them, Cheyenne continued.

"I appreciate you looking out for your friend, I really do, but I don't appreciate you insinuating that I just want to bag a SEAL. Jesus, Caroline, I've lived in

Riverton most of my life. You think any SEAL has ever *wanted* me before? It's not like I can pick one off the street like I'm ordering take out. I have no idea what Faulkner sees in me, and I'm still hoping he's serious and not just playing with me, but I can guaran-fucking-tee you that as long as he's interested in me, I'm his."

Cheyenne was breathing hard when she finished. She noticed Caroline was smiling at her. What the hell was she smiling about? She figured it out when an arm went around her waist, and one went around her chest and she was pulled back into a hard body. Faulkner.

"I'm interested in you, Shy."

Not looking behind her and not moving, Cheyenne looked at Caroline, who was no longer trying to hide her amusement and whispered, "Please tell me he didn't hear all of that."

"Sorry, Cheyenne, I think they *all* heard it."

Cheyenne closed her eyes as she heard the rustling of clothing and the quiet footsteps of more people joining them in the narrow hallway.

"Jesus Christ." She couldn't say anything else. All Faulkner's friends had heard her lose her shit on Caroline, the apparent matriarch of the group? Fuck.

"Okay, we're leaving now. Thanks for the meal, Ice. Wolf. I'll see the rest of you in the morning." Dude was all business. He shifted until Cheyenne was against his side and he put an arm around her waist, making sure she stayed there, and led her through the group of people now smiling at them.

"Bye, Cheyenne, it was nice meeting you."

"We'll call you soon!"

Cheyenne heard Caroline's voice say through her embarrassment. "We're having a girl's day out shopping soon, I'll call ya!"

The rest of the men added their goodbyes as well and Faulkner herded her out the front door to his truck. He opened the passenger door and got her seated and comfortable. Then Cheyenne watched as he rounded the front of the vehicle and got in next to her. Without a word, he started the car, did a U-turn in the middle of the road and drove down the street, presumably to his place.

Chapter Eight

CHEYENNE DIDN'T SAY anything on the trip to Faulkner's house. She was embarrassed beyond belief that Faulkner, and all his friends, had overheard her. She wasn't upset about *what* she'd said to Caroline though, every bit of that was dead-on true. She appreciated the fact Caroline was trying to protect her friend, but jeez, Caroline should've known by just looking at Cheyenne, she wasn't like that.

But knowing all of his friends, and Faulkner himself, had heard what she'd said was embarrassing as hell. Even now he hadn't said much to her. He'd been quiet all the way to his house. Cheyenne had half expected Faulkner to take her back to her own apartment and drop her off without a word, but he hadn't.

They pulled up to a small, well-kept brick house with only a small overhang over the front door. There was a long driveway which led to a one-car garage along the side and back of the house. The yard was well maintained, with no overgrown bushes lining the sides of the house, and the grass seemed to be freshly mowed.

Faulkner turned into the driveway and pulled to the end and shut off the truck. He didn't open the garage, simply got out and came around to Cheyenne's side of the vehicle. He helped her out, then opened the back door and grabbed her overnight bag from the back seat. Still without speaking, he put his hand on her waist and steered her to the back door. He put the key in the lock and led her inside.

They entered into a laundry room that had a basic washer and dryer in it. Without giving her a chance to look around, Faulkner all but pushed her through the small, but functional kitchen, and into the living room. Faulkner had a huge television mounted on the wall, not surprising, and a couch and love seat set in an L arrangement around a small coffee table.

The walls were a slight gray color that offset the dark browns of the couches. It was definitely a masculine looking room that fit Faulkner to a tee.

Still not stopping, Dude encouraged Cheyenne to keep walking. He steered her into a bedroom in the back of the house. Once he entered, Dude dropped her bag and turned Cheyenne in his arms until he was holding her upper arms and she was looking up at him.

"I'm sorry…"

Dude cut Cheyenne off before she could get anything else out. "Don't you fucking be sorry. You have no idea how much your words meant to me. I don't even know where to start. First, I'm pissed that Caroline had the nerve to try to warn you off."

"She loves you, she was looking out for you."

"I don't give a shit. It was rude. But, having said that, if she hadn't confronted you, you wouldn't have said what you did and I wouldn't have been there to hear it. I think your words are gonna stay with me forever. I knew you weren't thrilled to go over there tonight, but after we talked, I thought you were okay with it. But you weren't were you? You did it because you thought I wanted you to. You did it for me."

Looking at her, as if waiting for her agreement, Cheyenne gave a small nod.

"Yeah, you did it because you wanted to please me."

Again, when Faulkner didn't say anything else, Cheyenne nodded again, giving him the reassurance he needed. For once he didn't demand she say the words.

"You're into me. You said it. I heard it. All my friends heard it. I'm not letting you take it back."

"I don't want to take it back. I'm not an idiot, Faulkner. As much as you push me and boss me around, if I didn't want to be with you, I wouldn't be. If I didn't want to be standing in your bedroom right now, I wouldn't be here. I'm not a complete moron."

Cheyenne was fascinated at the affects her words were having on Faulkner. She could see his pupils dilate.

His fingers squeezed her biceps a bit harder and she saw him clench his teeth before he continued.

"You have no idea what I see in you."

Cheyenne just shook her head at him, agreeing. She had *no* idea what he saw in her.

"Jesus, Shy, it's everything. You're level headed, you're loyal, you're independent, you're humble and shy, but then you're all piss and vinegar when you have to be. You're a walking contradiction and it turns me on so much I can't stand it. But hearing you say you trust me? That you'd let me tie you to my bed? You have no idea what you've shared with me. I don't think you even understand your own needs, or mine, but I'm going to be there to help you figure it out. You said you were mine as long as I'm interested. Well, Shy, I'm interested and you're fucking mine."

Embarrassed, Cheyenne whispered, "Are you talking about BDSM?"

"Go sit on the bed, Shy," Dude ordered, not answering her question and dropping his hands from her arms and taking a step back.

"What?"

"Go sit on the bed. Do it."

Not understanding, Cheyenne took a step backward. Faulkner matched her steps. Every time she took a step back, he took a step forward. She took another, then another. Cheyenne kept her eyes on Faulkner's as she slowly backed into the room until the back of her legs hit the mattress. She sat, still looking up at Faulkner. Without thinking she brought her thumbnail up to her mouth and chewed on it. She was nervous as all hell. What was going on here?

"Not BDSM, Shy. Never that. I'm not down with labels. Who we are together is who we are. Nothing more, nothing less. But think about what just happened here. I asked you to do something and you did it. Why?"

Cheyenne thought about what he said. "I don't know."

"You know."

"Because you asked me to and I wanted to please you."

"Exactly. That's what this is about. I want to please you and you want to please me. We do that by me taking charge. It's what I need, and you submit to it so beautifully." Dude dropped to his haunches in front of her. He took the thumb Cheyenne had been chewing on and brought it to his mouth. "What'd I tell you I'd do if I caught you doing that again?" He waited for her to answer.

"That you'd do the same thing."

"Damn straight." Without looking away from Cheyenne's eyes, he took her thumb into his mouth. He nibbled on the pad, then wrapped his tongue around it.

He sucked, he caressed, he bit.

When he finally let go, Cheyenne felt boneless. "Seriously, is that supposed to be a deterrent, Faulkner? 'Cos I have to tell you, it's really not."

Dude chuckled at her words and wrapped his bad hand around hers. "Mine, Shy. You said it. I heard it. My friends heard it. Thank God I wasn't on a mission and was available to be there yesterday. Oh, someone else probably would've been able to disarm that bomb, but it wasn't someone else. It was me. We have this combustible connection that I've never felt before. We'll figure this out as we go. But I'm warning you, I don't think I'm going to lose interest in you anytime soon."

"Okay." It was all Cheyenne could think to say. It wasn't like she was going to argue with him.

"Okay. Here's how tonight will work. You get changed into whatever you've brought to sleep in. I know I told you I'd sleep on the couch tonight, but I don't think I can. I'll sleep in here with you. In my bed. Nothing will happen. I promised you that. You can trust me. I want you relaxed, and I want you to get used to me, to get more comfortable with me before we explore that part of our relationship. We'll get up in the morning, I'll make you breakfast then drive you home so you can get ready for your shift. We'll figure out the rest as we go."

Cheyenne noticed immediately that he wasn't asking. He was telling. She thought about it for a moment. Realizing she was okay with everything he'd said, she simply nodded as if Faulkner had actually asked for her approval.

He smiled and leaned over, bringing his mouth inches from hers. "You please me, Shy. Fuck, you please me. Now, go get changed."

Dude stood up and helped Cheyenne to her feet. He watched as she padded over to her bag, picked it up, and headed toward the little bathroom connected to the bedroom. The door closed behind her and Dude sagged onto the bed. Jesus, he was screwed. He'd barely known Cheyenne for a day and he was so far gone it wasn't funny. He'd always thought insta-love was a fallacy, something romance authors made up to sell books.

But he was knee deep in it. It was scary as hell, especially for someone used to being in control of every aspect of his life, but Dude welcomed it all the same. Sleeping next to Cheyenne, and not being inside her, would be one of the most difficult things he'd ever done, but he couldn't deny the thought of holding her in his arms all night sounded like heaven. He'd never, not once, spent the entire night with a woman. Oh, he'd catnapped and dozed after having sex, but he'd always woken up and left before the night had ended. Looking back, he knew it made him somewhat of an asshole, but it was the way he was and the way it had to be. But now, just the thought of holding Cheyenne in his arms all night felt right. Instead of the panicked feeling he usually got at the thought of having to deal with a woman "the morning after," Dude couldn't wait to see what Shy looked like first thing in the morning.

He left the bedroom, not wanting Cheyenne to feel awkward when she came out of the bathroom. Dude killed some time in the kitchen making sure he had what he needed for breakfast in the morning. Figuring he'd given Cheyenne enough time, he made his way back to his bedroom.

Seeing Cheyenne in his bed made him feel funny. He swallowed once, hard. Without a word he went into the bathroom. Knowing Cheyenne didn't have a direct line of sight into the room, he didn't bother closing the door. The room smelled like her. It smelled of toothpaste and some sort of sweet lotion. Dude took a closer look at the bottle on his counter, Gingerbread. Fuck. He'd never be able to think of Christmas again without thinking about her and her damn gingerbread lotion. Dude supposed it should have irritated him, her stuff strewn all over his counter, but instead it thrilled him.

He brushed his own teeth then stripped off his clothes down to his boxers. He usually slept nude, but knew that wasn't happening tonight. He probably should've pulled on a shirt, but Dude couldn't resist the thought of having Cheyenne close to his skin. He was pushing his control, but he couldn't stop himself.

He walked back into his bedroom to see Cheyenne lying on his bed and the covers up to her chin. She was obviously nervous and unsure.

Not wanting to prolong her anxiety, Dude strode across the room, turned off the light then turned back to the bed and pulled back the covers next to her. He climbed in and immediately turned over and pulled Cheyenne into him.

He arranged her so that she was up against his side, with her head resting on his shoulder. Dude put one hand around her and placed his other hand on her waist.

Dude relaxed when he felt Cheyenne's hand flatten against his chest. He relaxed further when he felt her muscles loosen and finally melt into him.

"Comfortable?"

"Surprisingly, yeah."

"Why surprisingly?"

"I've never spent the night with a guy before."

At Faulkner's sharp inhalation of breath, Cheyenne hurriedly explained. "No, Jesus, Faulkner, I'm not a virgin. Jeez. Relax. I just meant I've never slept in the same bed all night with a guy."

"I don't want to hear you talk about another man when you're in my arms and in my bed again, Shy, but just saying, they were idiots. I'm getting more satisfaction out of having you here in my arms and knowing you'll be here in the morning, just like this, than I ever have fucking a woman before."

Cheyenne propped herself up quickly and tried to glare at Faulkner in the darkness. "If I can't talk about other men, you can't talk about fucking any other women either," she snapped, irritated.

Chuckling, Dude raised his hand and soothed it over her back, feeling the soft cotton of her sleep shirt. "You're right, I'm sorry, Shy. I won't do it again."

"I mean, I know you've slept with a shit-ton of women, but I don't want to hear about them."

"It hasn't been a shit-ton."

"Whatever."

Dude chuckled. "All I meant, was that I've never felt as satisfied as I do right now, simply holding you."

"Good save." Cheyenne smiled. How could she stay mad at Faulkner when he said something like that?

"Go to sleep, Shy. I've got you."

"I know." After a moment Cheyenne whispered, "You didn't kiss me goodnight."

"I can't. If my mouth touches you, I'm lost. I'll taste whatever flavored lip shit you used, and it'll go straight to my head. It's bad enough I'm lying here smelling the gingerbread lotion you used tonight. I'm imaging how your skin will feel under me and how good you'll smell when I finally go down on you. If I even get a hint of

143

gingerbread mixed with your slick arousal, I'll lose it. So it might be a simple good night kiss to you, but it's a slippery slope that I'm holding on at the top of with my fingernails. So just shush and close your eyes. You'll get your kisses. I promise, Shy. Just not tonight, and not right now."

Giggling softly, Cheyenne simply said, "Okay."

"Sleep, Shy. For the love of God, close your eyes and sleep."

Dude lay in the dark waiting for Cheyenne to fall asleep. It didn't take long. The excitement of the last couple of days and the nervousness she'd felt tonight had obviously taken a toll on her.

Dude hadn't lied to her. Holding her in his arms was one of the most satisfying things he'd ever felt. Knowing she was just the kind of woman he needed and that Cheyenne wanted to please him was heady stuff. It wasn't just that he had a woman in his bed who Dude knew would be open to just about anything he wanted to do to her. It was that he had *Cheyenne* in his bed who would be open to anything he wanted to do to her. *That* was what made his control hard to hold on to. He never expected when he'd been called to a bomb threat that he'd meet his match, but Dude knew he'd spend the rest of his life thanking Christ he had.

When Cheyenne mumbled in her sleep, Dude clutched her closer to him and smiled as she quieted. He knew they'd moved really fast and he'd have to back off a bit so as not to scare her, but he wasn't going to let a day go by without making sure she knew he was thinking about her.

Chapter Nine

C HEYENNE SMILED AT the text message from Faulkner.

Thinking about you.

He never used shorthand when he texted her. He always spelled out every word and never used cute little emoticons in his messages. Not a day went by without him texting her at least once.

She thought back to their first morning together. She'd woken up and opened her eyes to see Faulkner staring down at her. She'd been on her back and he was propped up over her on an elbow. He'd taken her hair and smoothed it behind her ear.

"Morning, Shy."

"Good morning."

They'd just stared at each other, but when he'd lowered his head as if he was going to kiss her, Cheyenne sprang into action. There was no way she was letting him get near her with morning breath. She could feel how dry her mouth was. Yuck. When she'd explained, he'd merely laughed and let her up to head into the bathroom.

He'd cooked her breakfast as he'd promised. They'd spent a lazy morning together, getting to know each other better. Cheyenne found out Faulkner loved to read and had no issues reading romance books. He'd winked and told her it was "research."

When he'd dropped her off at her apartment, he'd kissed her long and hard. Cheyenne had decided on green apple lip balm that morning and she could tell how much he liked it by his reluctance to let her go. She smiled at the memory.

Then in typical Faulkner style, he'd simply held out his hand and demanded her cell phone. She'd unlocked it, given it to him, and watched as he programed in his numbers. He dialed his own phone and let it ring once, so he'd have her number as well.

He'd given it back, brought her lips to his once again with a hand at the back of her neck, given her one more deep kiss then let her go.

"I'll talk to you later," and he was gone.

Faulkner had been true to his word. She'd gotten several texts from him during her shift. He demanded she let him know when she got home. He didn't like the thought of her going home at eleven at night.

Cheyenne just rolled her eyes at his demanding text.

She'd been working second shift for so long, the late night hours didn't faze her anymore. She told Faulkner as much, but he merely told her that while she might not care that criminals tended to be more active and would troll for victims when the sun went down, but *he* did.

While she might pretend it annoyed her, deep down Cheyenne knew she was lying to herself. She loved that Faulkner was worried about her. It felt good.

Over the last two weeks their schedules were out of sync, so they hadn't been able to spend the night together again. It had worried Cheyenne until Faulkner reassured her.

"I don't care if it's a year before we're able to get together, Shy, you're mine. We have all the time in the world. Stop worrying about it."

Thinking about his words could still make her tingle and feel better, no matter what was going on in her life.

Cheyenne needed his text today more than usual. She'd talked to her mom that morning and heard all about how Karen had been involved in a big case that had won in court. Her mom had bragged about Karen for twenty minutes straight before even bothering to ask Cheyenne about how her day went.

When Cheyenne had told her how she'd helped a man deliver a baby after he'd called the emergency line, her mom had actually said, "Cheyenne, when are you going to get a real job?"

Cheyenne had merely sighed and listened absently until her mom had finally said she had to go. She was meeting Karen for lunch. It always hurt knowing her mom and Karen got together regularly, and never bothered to invite Cheyenne.

So looking at the three words on her cell phone from Faulkner made her feel good.

Miss u 2. :)

Cheyenne put her phone aside when the phone on the console in front of her rang.

"911, what is your emergency?"

The voice on the other end of the phone sounded completely calm, which was highly unusual. "Yes, I'm looking for a Cheyenne who works as a 911 operator."

Cheyenne frowned. What the hell? She couldn't tell if the person on the other end of the line was a man or a woman, it was muffled and soft.

"Do you have an emergency? This line is for emergencies only."

Cheyenne heard a dial tone in her ear. She shivered. That was really weird. She didn't really keep her job a secret, but she'd never had someone ask for her specifically when they'd called. She tried to see if she could see what number the call had come from, but the person hadn't stayed on the line long enough and they were using a cell phone. The data simply wasn't available.

Her cell phone dinged with a text message.

I'm picking you up after work tonight.

Forgetting the weird call, Cheyenne snatched up her phone excitedly.

Don't u have pt in the am?
I don't care.
But u'll be tired
I said I don't care. This has gone on too long. I need to see you.

Cheyenne smiled happily. She needed to see Faulkner too. They'd gotten to know each other pretty well over the last two weeks. He'd call when she was working and they'd chat until she had to answer the emergency line. Faulkner never cared that she'd have to hang up with him immediately when that happened. He'd merely told her to text when she was done and could talk again.

It'd worked out really well. Cheyenne had found out all sorts of things about Faulkner and about his friends. She loved how loyal he was and how loyal it seemed his friends were back with him. She learned that he liked to cook, but hated to do laundry. He admitted he'd read his first romance novel as a dare by Caroline, and that he'd actually enjoyed it.

Cheyenne had shared about her mom and sister and how she'd always felt second fiddle to them, then had to listen to a lecture from Faulkner about how wrong they were and how he and all his friends thought she was an amazing human being.

Talking with Faulkner always made her smile.

Cheyenne would always remember the conversation they'd had one night after she'd gotten home from her shift. She'd uncharacteristically texted him to see if he was awake. She typically didn't like to wake him up late at night because she knew he had to get up so early, but she'd had a horrible phone call and desperately wanted to talk to him.

He'd texted back immediately and told her to call him.

"What's wrong, Shy?"

"I just…I had a hard night."

"What happened?"

"Just a call."

"It's never *just* a call, not if it upsets you. Tell me."

"I probably should let you go, you have to get up in like, three hours."

"Cheyenne…"

Not able to resist him when he used *that* tone of voice, and knowing she honestly really did want to talk to Faulkner about it, she told him.

"A woman called, hysterical. She went into her

twelve year old son's room to check on him and found him hanging in his closet. He'd wrapped a belt around his neck and killed himself."

"Oh, Shy..."

Faulkner's sympathy almost broke her, but she continued quickly. "She told me he'd been quiet lately. She knew he was struggling at school. Seventh grade is tough on all kids I think. I know I hated it, and myself, most of the time. She said she was a single mom and hadn't had the time to check in with him lately, not the way she should've. He was gay and had told his mom that some of the other kids had been picking on him. She blamed herself, Faulkner. She said that it was all her fault. I talked to her until the paramedics got there and tried to revive her son. By what she'd told me I knew he was probably already gone, but I kept her busy until help arrived. She didn't want to hang up with me. She wanted to tell me all about how great her son had been. She said he was an artist and wanted to grow up to work in animation. It wasn't until the police told her she had to hang up and talk with them, that she finally let me go." Cheyenne had sniffed once. "It was tough."

"She'll never forget you were there for her though."

"I'll never understand people as long as I live, Faulkner," Cheyenne complained sadly. "Here was this kid, full of potential, a good kid, and other people made him feel like he was less of a person just because of his sexual orientation. Less worthy. It's just not right. It's not fair."

"Listen to yourself, Shy. *Hear* what you just said."

Cheyenne stilled.

Dude continued, hoping she was really hearing him. "Your sister has done that to you her entire life. And now even your mom does it, knowingly or not. They put you down and make you feel like what you do for a living isn't as important as what Karen does."

"Holy shit, Faulkner, you're right."

"Of course I am."

Cheyenne chuckled, in spite of the heavy conversation they'd been having. "Thank you, I needed that."

"I know, baby. I'm sorry you had to go through that, but don't ever think I'd rather sleep than listen to you and help you work through a tough call. I'll be pissed if you do it after tonight. Got me?"

"Got you." She'd hung up and slept soundly that night. Usually after a tough call she tossed and turned most of the night reliving it over and over.

Cheyenne startled when her cell phone buzzed in her hand. She'd been so lost in her thoughts of the past, she hadn't texted Faulkner back.

We'll figure out your car later. I'll be there at 11:10. Is that enough time?

Cheyenne quickly typed out a response.

Y, can't wait

Cheyenne couldn't wait until the end of her shift. While she'd enjoyed getting to know Faulkner over the last couple of weeks via texts and phone calls, she was more than ready to see him in person again. She didn't know if he was just giving her time to get used to him or if he really had been busy, but at this point she didn't really care.

She really hoped the chemistry they'd had before hadn't waned. She didn't think it had, but what did she know about men like Faulkner?

Cheyenne sat back and drummed her fingers on the tabletop. Only two hours to go until her shift was over.

Chapter Ten

CHEYENNE WAVED TO David, her relief operator, and headed out the door. Faulkner had texted her ten minutes ago to say he was outside and ready whenever she was.

She'd closed up her station and explained what had gone on that night to David. Luckily, so far it had been pretty quiet, all things considered. She put her purse over her shoulder and pushed out into the dark parking lot.

Faulkner was parked under one of the lights in the lot and was standing outside leaning against the passenger door of his truck. Cheyenne walked toward him with a wide happy smile on her face.

Suddenly feeling shy, and not really knowing why, they'd talked on the phone almost every day, but it was different being face to face with Faulkner again. It was much easier to bare your soul to someone when you weren't looking them in the eyes.

"Hey."

"Hey. The night go okay?"

Cheyenne loved that Faulkner always asked about how her shift went. "It was good, kinda boring actually."

"Boring is good."

Cheyenne nodded in agreement.

"Come here."

Cheyenne shivered at the tone of Faulkner's voice, and went to him.

Dude wrapped his arms around Cheyenne and breathed her in. Tonight she smelled like vanilla. He smiled at her penchant to wear sweet food-smelling lotion.

"I wonder what flavor your lips are tonight." Without giving her a chance to answer, Dude leaned down and stole the kiss he'd been desperate for since the last time he'd kissed Cheyenne. He ran his tongue over her lips, tasting cherry, before plunging into her mouth. She opened willingly to him and Dude loved feeling her hands grab onto the back of his shirt as he continued his sensual assault.

Before he could go too far, he pulled back. "Cherry. Yum." Dude watched as Cheyenne's lips quirked up into a smile and she turned her head to the side adorably. "Let's go, it wouldn't do to get caught necking in the parking lot of a public service building."

Cheyenne looked up at Faulkner again and simply

nodded. He reached over and opened the door for her and once again waited until she'd settled in the seat before shutting the door and walked around to the driver's side.

"Where are we going?"

"Your place."

Cheyenne wasn't expecting that. "Mine?"

"Yeah. Yours. You don't have any of your stuff, so we'll go there, you can pack, then we'll go back to my house."

"Why don't we just stay at my apartment tonight? If we're already there…" Her words tapered off at the look Faulkner was giving her, then she asked, "What?"

"Because the first time I make love to you will be in my bed, in my house. I've been dreaming about seeing you splayed out on my sheets waiting for me. I've jacked off to the thought of you in my space the entire time we've been apart. I'm done waiting. You're mine, and you'll be mine tonight in every way possible."

Cheyenne just stared at him. Wow. That was intense. She loved it. She smiled. "Okay, Faulkner, whatever you say."

He smiled back. "Get used to saying those words, Shy. I fucking love hearing them come from your lips."

Cheyenne wasn't surprised when Faulkner leaned over to her and captured her lips again for one more intense kiss before he pulled back and started the truck.

He pulled out of the lot and headed toward her apartment, leaving three cars sitting in the parking lot, one of which wasn't empty.

FAULKNER HAD WALKED her up to her apartment and stood in the living room while she packed. It didn't take her long, but Cheyenne made sure to pack a couple of outfits. She was off for the next few days and didn't know what Faulkner had planned. She figured it'd be better to be safe than sorry.

She walked out of her bedroom and said, "Sorry it took so long, I'm ready."

Faulkner didn't come toward her, just stood next to her window looking out. He turned when she spoke and simply looked at her. Finally he said, "Be sure about this, Shy. Be sure it's what you want and not something you're doing because I want it."

"I've never been more sure of anything in my entire life, Faulkner."

"Then come on, let's go."

The ride to Faulkner's house was quiet, but electric.

Finally when they were a block from his house, Dude broke the comfortable, but intense, silence. "When we get home, go into the house. I'll give you five minutes before I follow you. Make sure you do what you need to in the bathroom. When I get there, I want to see you in my bed, naked, covers pulled back, not covering you. Lie on your back with your arms over your head. Keep your head turned toward the door so you'll see me the second I walk in. Don't speak. Do you have any questions or concerns before we get there?"

Cheyenne felt her nipples peak at his words. My God, Faulkner was completely one hundred percent serious. This was really going to happen, and it was going to happen his way. Cheyenne tried not to hyperventilate. "Will I get a safe word?"

"Fuck no," his response was immediate. "You don't need a safe word. You don't like something, just tell me. I told you I'm not into games. But I promise you, Shy, you'll like everything we do. I'm not into pain, yours or mine. If you need to stop me, I'm not doing it right." He paused a beat. "Anything else?"

Cheyenne shook her head.

"Words."

"No, Faulkner. I'm good. I'm so good, I'm about ready to go off without you even touching me."

Cheyenne saw Faulkner smile quickly, a small satisfied smile, before he banked it and ordered. "Don't. You don't come until I say you can."

"Jesus," Cheyenne muttered under her breath.

The cab of the truck was silent until Faulkner stopped the truck in his driveway.

"Go on, Shy. Five minutes. Remember what I said."

Dude watched as Cheyenne headed into his house, her bag over her shoulder. He'd given her his key and she didn't hesitate for one single second to take it and make her way quickly through the door. Dude put his head on the steering wheel.

The past two weeks had been hell. He'd made up reasons why they couldn't get together in person. He'd done everything he could to try to slow things down, to really get to know Cheyenne and to have her get to know him. Two weeks really wasn't a long time in most normal relationships, but this one didn't seem "normal" to him. He felt deep in his gut that Cheyenne was meant to be his. They were both in the right place at the right time to meet. Dude hadn't believed much in fate before, even after seeing his friends and teammates find the women of their dreams in the most unusual of ways. The two weeks apart had given Dude a good understanding of what made Cheyenne the person she was today, and made him fall for her all the more.

When he'd heard about how her mom and sister treated her, he'd wanted to march over to their houses and give them a piece of his mind. The only thing that stopped him, was that he knew Cheyenne would've been embarrassed if he'd followed through.

Dude had opened up to Cheyenne about his likes and dislikes, and he honestly felt as if they'd becoming closer as a result. His libido hadn't liked it, but Dude *did* like the feeling of this relationship being different from the others he'd had. In the past he hadn't wanted to get to know a woman before taking her to bed. All he'd cared about was getting her off, then getting himself off. With Cheyenne, he didn't want to take her to his bed until he knew more about her and what made her tick.

She was sensitive and shy. Passionate and repressed. Emotional and closed off. She was a mass of contradictions and she absolutely fascinated him.

Dude looked at his watch. Two minutes to go. He opened his door, shut it behind him and pressed "lock" on his key fob. He leaned against the door with his feet crossed at the ankles. Tonight would be telling. He hoped like hell Cheyenne would enjoy it.

If she didn't, then they had no future. It was that simple. Dude was the way he was. He'd been honest with her. He wasn't into games, or pain, or the other crap that came with what people thought the BDSM lifestyle was about. He'd read some of Caroline's erotic romances. Some were all right, but it wasn't for him. He didn't need the kneeling, serving, and floggers, but he *did* need the control. Knowing a woman trusted him to let him lead their lovemaking was heady and was what excited him.

From what Dude had seen, Cheyenne needed him to be in control too. She took too much on herself.

Between her job, her family, and her independent lifestyle, the few times he'd taken control, she'd melted in his arms.

He looked at his watch again. One minute. He pushed off the truck and headed toward his house. He'd never been so excited, or hard, in his life. He was ready to take what was his.

Chapter Eleven

CHEYENNE LAY ON Faulkner's bed and waited. She could feel her heart beating quickly. She knew her breathing had increased. She gripped the slats of Faulkner's bed frame so hard, she figured her knuckles were probably white. He hadn't told her to grab hold of them, but when Cheyenne had seen the bed again, she couldn't stop thinking about being tied to it.

She worried about her body, would Faulkner like it? Most of the time in the past when she'd had sex, the room had been dark and the men hadn't bothered to try to check her out all that much before they'd gone for the gusto.

Cheyenne had turned on the light in the bedroom and decided to leave it on. She'd used the restroom and slicked herself up with her gingerbread lotion, remembering his words from two weeks ago. She swiped her lips with her favorite flavor, cake batter, and tore her clothes off. Not bothering to look at herself in the mirror, she'd rushed into Faulkner's bedroom to make sure she was in place when her five minutes was up.

Faulkner was right. Cheyenne wanted to please him. He'd asked her to do something and she wanted nothing more than to follow his directions to the letter. She knew that in pleasing Faulkner, she too would be satisfied.

Not knowing how much time had passed, Cheyenne kept her eyes on the bedroom door. The last thing she wanted was to be caught not looking when Faulkner walked in. Besides, she wanted to see his first unguarded reaction when he saw her.

She clenched the slats of the bed above her head. How much time had gone by anyway? The anticipation was killing her.

Then Faulkner was there. His eyes bore into hers as he entered the room. Cheyenne kept her mouth shut, he'd ordered her not to talk. She knew she was breathing too fast, but she was nervous as hell. Cheyenne bit her lip, trying to keep any words back. Faulkner was intense and beautiful, and all hers.

She watched as he stalked, yes stalked, across the room until he stood over her.

"Nice touch with the slats, Shy. Don't let go until I tell you to."

Cheyenne smiled up at him and nodded, thankful he'd noticed her efforts.

"Wonder what flavor you're wearing tonight?"

The question was rhetorical since Cheyenne knew he didn't want her to speak. She waited for him to take her lips, and pouted when he didn't.

Instead he leaned down and put his nose in her belly button. He didn't touch her anywhere else, but Cheyenne sucked in a breath all the same.

He breathed in and stood up again. "Fuck me. Gingerbread. You wear that for me?"

Cheyenne nodded, not taking her eyes off Faulkner.

"God. Fucking perfect."

Cheyenne watched as Faulkner unbuttoned his shirt slowly. One button at a time. Cheyenne couldn't help but squirm on the bed.

"Still, Shy."

Cheyenne immediately stilled. Crap. It was harder than it seemed. She'd always scoffed at the women in her books that would whimper and moan when their men told them to stay still. She was just realizing how much harder it was than it seemed to be still. Those authors obviously knew what they were talking about.

Cheyenne sucked in a breath when Faulkner sat next to her on the bed, still wearing his pants, but devoid of his shirt. Her eyes eagerly roamed over him. He was built. She knew he worked out every morning with his team, but Jesus, she'd never seen an eight pack before.

"You like the feel of my hand don't you, Shy?"

She nodded immediately, lying. She didn't like it,

she loved it.

"Let's test that shall we?"

Cheyenne sucked in a breath as Faulkner went right for the kill. He didn't mess around by touching her stomach or shoulders or face. He went right for her breasts, and her nipples that were drawn up into hard peaks. He rubbed his scarred fingers over her breasts until Cheyenne thought her heart was going to beat out of her chest.

She opened her mouth to plead with Faulkner to do something, and at the last second remembered. She shut her mouth.

"Perfect. Thank you for trying so hard. I love watching your restraint."

Dude brought his index finger to her lips and rubbed against them, smearing her lip balm over his finger. He smirked at her and brought his finger down and rubbed the balm he'd pilfered from her lips over her nipple, then leaned down. Cheyenne tensed, she'd wanted his lips on her again since the first night. She'd dreamed about it.

Faulkner nipped and sucked and completely drove her crazy. He brought his hand up and continued to torture the first nipple as he moved his mouth to the other. Finally he covered both her breasts with his hands. Cheyenne could feel her nipples stabbing into his palms. He rubbed and caressed her as he spoke.

"Is that cake?"

Cheyenne just smirked at him.

"Oh, I'm going to like this game. I wonder how many different flavors you have? We could really have fun with them. But I think I need a different taste in my mouth now."

Dude tried to still his racing heart. When he'd walked into the room and saw Cheyenne had followed his directions to the letter, and then some, he'd almost lost it right there. She was fucking beautiful. She was a feast to his senses.

Taking his time, he slid to the end of the bed, never losing eye contact with Cheyenne. He positioned himself between her legs and slowly slid them further apart. "Bend." He tapped her knees and smiled as she immediately bent her legs until he could lie down comfortably between them.

"I hope you're comfortable, Shy. I plan on spending a lot of time down here." Dude leaned down and inhaled. "Oh yeah. Gingerbread and you. There's nothing better."

He got to work driving his woman crazy. Bringing her to the edge and pulling back over and over again, Dude knew Cheyenne was going to orgasm like she never had before. He looked up at her, not slowing his fingers as they continued to caress and tease her.

"Look at me."

Waiting until Cheyenne's eyes drifted down and met his, Dude continued. "You've been so good, Shy. So fucking responsive. You've done everything I've asked. You followed my directions to the letter. I've never been more pleased before. *Never.* Let go. As many times as you can. For me. No words, but don't hold back your reactions either. I want to hear you."

As soon as the words left his mouth, he leaned down and sucked on her bud, hard. Cheyenne exploded. It was as if she was waiting for his explicit permission. She cried out in delight and arched her back, riding his fingers. Dude rode out Cheyenne's first orgasm and built her up to another. She bucked and moaned, but didn't speak. She was amazing.

Dude regretfully pulled his finger out of her snug sheath and leaned down for one more long lick. He felt Cheyenne shudder under him. He couldn't wait anymore. He had to have her. She was still twitching and Dude hoped she'd have at least one more orgasm left in her.

"Legs down."

As soon as Cheyenne dropped her legs bonelessly to the bed, Dude shifted until he straddled her hips. He unbuckled his jeans and eased the zipper down carefully. He watched as Cheyenne licked her lips. He looked down and the head of his dick was peeking out the top waistband of his boxers. He wasn't surprised. He'd been harder than he ever had been before in his life for the last half hour.

Meeting Cheyenne's eyes again he said, "Eyes on mine, Shy." He chuckled as she reluctantly brought her eyes up to his. "You'll get to see it all you want in a moment. But for now, keep your eyes on mine."

Dude eased off the bed and quickly shucked his pants and boxers off. He opened the drawer to the nightstand next to the bed, and grabbed a condom, all without breaking eye contact with her. He opened the wrapper without looking, and covered himself with the latex. He resumed his position on the bed over Cheyenne, but this time got on his hands and knees. He lowered himself just enough so that the only part of him that was touching her was his manhood.

"Feel that?" he whispered, "It's all I can do not to plunge into you with one stroke. To fill you up so completely you don't know where you end and I begin."

Dude watched as Cheyenne's eyes dilated until he could barely see the brown color of her irises anymore. "You want that?"

He watched as Cheyenne nodded frantically. He teased her a bit more. "You sure?" When she nodded again and licked her lips, Dude asked, "Maybe you're tired?"

As she shook her head desperately he said seriously, "What you do to me, Shy. I can't wait anymore. I thought I could tease you some more, but I can't. I need to be in you." With that, Dude lowered himself and fit himself to her core and pushed. He drove inside her until it was just as he'd told her *she'd* feel. He didn't know where he ended and she began.

She was hot and wet and felt better than anything Dude had ever experienced before.

"Please," Cheyenne croaked out. "I want to touch you."

Not caring or reprimanding her for speaking, Dude groaned, "Yes, God yes."

At his words, Cheyenne loosened her grip on his bed slats and drove one hand into Faulkner's hair, and the other gripped the muscles on his back.

"Oh God, Faulkner. I can't keep quiet anymore. Please don't make me."

"Whatever you need, Shy. Whatever you need."

"I need you. I need you to move. I need your hands on me. You feel so good. God, you have no idea. I've never...I mean no one has ever...Fuck. I can't think. You're so hard, everywhere. I have no idea why you want me, but I'm here, I'm yours. Jesus, Faulkner. Yes." It as if being allowed to speak again broke a dam inside her. Her words spewed out without thought, but with extreme emotion.

Dude's thrusts got harder the longer she spoke. It was obvious she wasn't thinking, just speaking what she felt. Dude never felt more like a man.

"Yes, Shy, tell me what you need."

"You. I need you. Harder. Please. It feels so good. Yessssss."

Dude kept his eyes open and watched Cheyenne's face. Her eyes were scrunched up tight and her head was thrown back. She was moaning and squirming in his arms as she bucked up against him even as he thrust into her. Cheyenne held on to him tightly and never let go, even when he thrust especially hard, she was right there with him.

Her eyes finally popped open and looked him in the eyes. "Faulkner, Fuck. Yes. I'm going to…"

Dude reached down and rubbed his thumb over her clit, hard. All it took was two hard strokes and she exploded again. Dude gritted his teeth against the feeling of her inner muscles clenching rhythmically against him and her body twitching and bucking up against him. He held his orgasm back by the skin of his teeth and when Cheyenne stopped quivering against him, he put both hands on either side of her head and growled, "Look at me, Shy. Watch yourself take me over the edge. Watch what you do to me. You. Only you."

Cheyenne felt boneless. She opened her eyes at Faulkner's demand and watched his face as he thrust into her. She saw the second his release came over him. He thrust against her once, twice, then after the third hard thrust, stayed buried to the hilt. His eyes never fully closed, but did shut into slits. Cheyenne watched as the vein in Faulkner's neck throbbed and he gritted his teeth and grunted. It was sexy as hell and she'd done this to him. Cheyenne brought a hand up to Faulkner's neck and gripped him tightly.

Finally the muscles in his body lost their rigid tone and he blew out a breath. "Jesus, fuck."

"I think that's my line," Cheyenne teased dreamily.

Dude collapsed onto Cheyenne's chest with a grunt. He heard her squeak in surprise and then felt her arms go around his back and pull him into her. He was never letting her go. Never.

Chapter Twelve

What r u up 2 2day?

We have a meeting with our commander then we have more PT.

U always have pt.

Yeah, and you love the results.

Ok that's true. :)

Cheyenne smiled as she texted Faulkner. He was so funny. She loved talking to him this way. Somehow it seemed more intimate and made her feel closer to him. The last month had been a dream. They didn't get to spend the night with each other every night because of their schedules, but when they did, they made the most of it.

What are you doing today?

Lunch w/ mom and sis.

I wish you would wait until I could go with you.

I'll b ok.

Wait until I can go with you.

Sorry, that only wrks in bed.

Damn. Thought I'd give it a try.

Laughing out loud and ignoring the funny looks she was getting from the people around her in the coffee shop, Cheyenne continued to text.

It's only lnch. I'll text when done.

Call me instead. I want to hear your voice to know you are okay.

I'll b fine.

Call. Me.

Oh ok mr. bossy.

Later

Ltr

Cheyenne turned her phone off and put it in her bag. She sat back waiting for her family to arrive. She'd purposely picked the little coffee shop, knowing her sister would hate it. She wasn't proud of herself, but she rationalized at least this way their lunch would be kept short.

She stood up as Karen and her mom walked into the shop. Karen looked impeccable as always. She was wearing a brown skirt that was a proper knee length. She'd paired it with a white button up shirt and a brown suit jacket. She was wearing brown heels and had her hair up in a complicated looking twist.

Cheyenne's mom was just as put together. Dressed in a pair of gray slacks with a pale pink angora short sleeve sweater, a pair of low heels, and her hair up in a bun, the gray in her hair matched the pants she was wearing perfectly.

Cheyenne felt frumpy next to her family, but shook off the feeling. It was her day off. She wasn't going to worry about dressing up. The jeans, fitted T-shirt, and flip-flops she was wearing were fine. She'd put her hair up in a ponytail to keep it out of her face.

"Hey Mom, Karen."

"Cheyenne, how many times do I have to tell you to take more care with your appearance?"

Cheyenne sighed. No "hello," no "how are you doing," her mom just jumped right in with the criticisms. Nothing ever changed. "Mom, it's my day off…"

Her mom cut her off. "That's no excuse. You never know who you'll run into while you are out and about and it pays to look your best. Look at your sister. She always looks impeccable. How do you expect to attract a man if you don't put any effort in?"

"Actually…"

Cheyenne was cut off again, this time by her sister.

"I can't believe the news isn't sick of your little incident yet. I mean really. I think a month and a half is enough already."

Cheyenne looked at Karen in bewilderment, forgetting she was about to tell her mom that she *had* attracted a man, a hell of a man. "What are you talking about?"

"You didn't know? There was another special on you last night. Well, at least on what happened. I don't know why you won't just talk to the press already. It would probably get them off your back."

"*Another* special?" Cheyenne didn't know what her sister was talking about.

"Yeah. *Another* special. The news station has done a couple of shows highlighting the various people that were involved in what happened. They highlighted all of the guys the police killed, and touched on you. They weren't allowed to talk about the military guy that was involved though. I felt kinda bad for the men that were killed. They all had families and such sad backgrounds."

Cheyenne couldn't believe what she was hearing. "Are you shitting me?"

Her mom immediately rebuked, "Cheyenne, watch your language."

Cheyenne turned to her. "Are *you* shitting me?"

"Cheyenne Nicole Cotton, language," her mom scolded her again.

Cheyenne turned back to Karen. "I can't believe you said that. You're supposed to be my *sister*. My flesh and blood. Do you know what they *did* to me?"

"You look okay to me. Jeez, Cheyenne, you've always been such a drama queen."

Cheyenne shook her head and leaned toward her sister. "I invited you guys today because I wanted to try to get to know you better. I've always felt bad we didn't get along. But I can't believe you'd say something like that to a stranger, nonetheless your own flesh and blood. Those men you are busy feeling sorry for, *hit* me. They threatened me with guns. They scared the crap out of me. They strapped a fucking *bomb* to my chest and wouldn't have thought twice about blowing me to bits. And you have the gall to sit there and tell me about how you feel bad for *their* families? That they had such hard lives that what they did was okay? The next thing you're going to say is that you think the cops were in the wrong for shooting them."

"I do," Karen immediately returned, a hateful look in her eye.

Cheyenne nodded once. She calmly put her napkin on the table in front of her.

"Look, maybe we…" her mother began.

Cheyenne interrupted her mother. "I'm done. You're cold, Karen. I have no idea how you got that way, but you are. I don't know what I did to you to make you hate me so much, except for being born, and I don't think I can take any blame for *that*. All I've ever wanted is a big sister I could hang out with and look up to, but you never gave me a chance. I don't want to see or talk to you again. If you have more sympathy for a bunch of thugs than your own sister, you're no family of mine."

It wasn't Karen that spoke up, but her mom. "Cheyenne, you can't do that. You don't mean it."

"What do *you* think, Mom? Do you feel sorry for those guys too?"

"Well, it wasn't as if the police gave them a chance to give up did they?"

"I'm done with you too," Cheyenne whispered immediately, tears gathering in her eyes. "All my life I've tried to be good enough. I've done everything I could think of to make you feel a fraction of pride toward me as you do for Karen. But it's obvious you don't and can't. So that's fine. Don't call me again. Just leave me alone."

Turning on her heel, Cheyenne left the coffee shop. She beeped her car doors open and climbed in on autopilot. She wasn't surprised when she didn't see either her mom or Karen storm out of the coffee shop in pursuit of her. They were probably inside gossiping about her and reassuring each other that they'd said nothing wrong.

Cheyenne drove to the beach. She'd always loved the sound of the waves against the sand. It usually relaxed her, but not today.

She'd had no idea the media was airing "specials"

about what had happened to her. She felt sick inside about the spin they were putting on the men who'd taken her and the two other women hostage. They'd terrorized her. Cheyenne honestly thought she was going to die and it had scared the shit out of her.

To think there were people who felt *sorry* for those men was sickening. That her own flesh and blood felt sorry for the men, was disheartening and made her feel more alone than she'd ever felt before.

Cheyenne sat facing the ocean on the stone wall that lined the parking lot. She'd been so happy. She'd just spent the last four nights in Faulkner's bed and every single night, that week and when they'd been together in the past month, he'd made her body hum. He'd shown her how good "submitting" to him could be. She trusted him with her life.

Just when things were starting to look up for her, her own damn family had to ruin it. She should've known Karen would be jealous of the media attention she was getting, even though Cheyenne had always refused to speak to the press.

Cheyenne should've waited for Faulkner to have lunch with her family. She'd honestly thought she could work on repairing their relationship though. It was her *mom*. Moms were supposed to love all their kids equally, but *her* mom never had.

Pulling her feet up onto the wall in front of her,

Cheyenne linked her arms around her shins and put her cheek to her knees. How long she sat like that she had no idea, but eventually her butt went numb and she had to move. Stiffly she released her legs and let them fall to the ground. She wasn't ready to leave yet, but knew she'd better get in touch with Faulkner. He'd wanted her to call him when she was done with lunch, but Cheyenne hadn't wanted to talk to him, or anyone else.

She walked to her car and grabbed her phone out of her purse. She walked back toward the beach and set off down the sidewalk until she got to a part of the beach that wasn't as crowded. She kicked off her flip-flops and wandered into the sand. Finding a place that seemed as good as any, she sank down.

She turned on the screen to her phone and winced. Three texts and a phone message. All from Falkner. The fact that even with what she'd said, neither her sister nor her mom had tried to get a hold of her, cut deep.

She looked at the texts first.

Just checking in. How was lunch?
I haven't heard from you. Call me.
CALL ME.

Somehow, even though it was written, she could sense Faulkner's irritation with her. Cheyenne really didn't want to listen to the voice mail from him. He was probably pissed at her. She couldn't deal with someone else being pissed at her.

Scrolling through her contacts, Cheyenne hesitated over Caroline's number, then clicked "send message."

One night after dinner, Faulkner had taken her cell and programmed in all his teammates numbers. He'd even added in all of the women as well. She'd protested, telling Faulkner that she didn't even know them, but he'd ignored her and done it anyway.

Then, bizarrely, he'd pointed to one name he'd put in her phone and told her seriously, "If you are *ever* in trouble and can't get a hold of me, call Tex."

"Tex? Who is that? Is that another nickname for one of your teammates?"

"Tex is a former SEAL who lives in Virginia. He can find anyone. It's a long story, but suffice it to say, he's had a hand in helping us protect all of my friends' women at one time or another. I'd trust him with my life. He's got connections we can't hope to have. Just promise. Okay?"

She had.

But this wasn't a situation where she wanted to talk to a stranger, and she wasn't in trouble. She just needed a friend. She quickly typed out a text.

Hey Caroline, it's Cheyenne. U around?

The response came almost immediately.

Hey C. what's up?

Suddenly Cheyenne didn't know what to say. She didn't know why she'd texted Caroline in the first place.

Cheyenne? U ok?

Yeah. Got a sec to talk? Can I call?

Of course.

Cheyenne took a deep breath. She had to start somewhere. She liked Caroline and the other women and she needed a friend. She hit Caroline's number and waited for her to pick up.

"Hey, Cheyenne."

"Hey."

"Seriously, are you okay?"

"Yeah. I need some advice."

"Let me guess, about a certain SEAL we both know?"

"Yeah." Cheyenne let out her breath. "I think he's mad at me," she whispered, not knowing why she was whispering.

"What'd you do?"

"I was supposed to call him, and didn't. He sent three texts and the last one was all capital letters."

Caroline laughed. When Cheyenne didn't join in, she sobered. "Hey, you're serious aren't you? Look, I piss Matthew off all the time, but he gets over it."

"I don't want Faulkner to yell at me," Cheyenne's breath hitched. "I've had a bad day. But the longer I wait to call him, I know the madder he'll get."

"Where are you? You aren't home are you?"

"No. I'm sitting on a beach watching the sun go down because I'm a wuss. I can't go home because he'll find me and yell at me. He's…he's bossy. And I…fuck. This is embarrassing."

"I get it, Cheyenne. We all know Faulkner is a lot more intense about his bossiness than the other guys are. But, Shy, he won't yell at you if he knows you've had a bad day."

"Everything has been so good between us. I like the way he is…the way we are…I don't want to ruin it."

"Listen to me. These SEALS are intense. They're big, bad, and brash, but as I told you when you were at my house, inside they're big teddy bears. All you have to do is be honest with him. Tell Faulkner that you're sorry you didn't call but you needed some time. Then apologize for it and let him make your day better."

When Cheyenne didn't say anything Caroline continued. "Oh, Shy. What happened?"

"I…don't…I can't…"

"Okay, you don't have to tell me. But please, let Faulkner know where you are. He's probably worried sick about you. It's how they are. Do you want me to call him?"

"No, I'll do it. I just needed…a pep talk I guess."

"I'm so glad you called me. Seriously. Call me anytime you need to. I can't promise to be able to explain half the things these guys do, but we can at least put our heads together and try to figure it out. And just so you know, when the guys get sent out on a mission, we all get together and get completely drunk the first night. It's our own brand of a support group."

Cheyenne giggled, as she supposed Caroline meant for her to.

"And we're still going shopping one of these days. I promise to get the girls together sooner rather than later. Okay? You'll come with us?"

"Yeah, I think I'd like that. Thanks."

"Okay. Cheyenne? Call Faulkner and let him know where you are. Trust him to take care of you. It sounds like you already trust him to do so at home…"

Cheyenne knew what Caroline was getting at, and blushed.

"Trust him in the light of day too. He needs that from you."

"Okay. Thanks, Caroline."

"Anytime. I'll talk to you soon."

"Okay, Bye."

"Bye."

Cheyenne clicked the end button and stared down at her phone. The message waiting icon mocked her. She couldn't do it. She couldn't listen to Faulkner's message right now.

Arguing with herself for a good five minutes, Cheyenne finally bit her lip and opened the text app. She needed to at least text him.

Hey. Sry I didn't call

The response was almost immediate.

Where are you?

I'm ok.

Shy, where are u? I'm worried about u.

Cheyenne looked at the latest message from Faulkner. He'd used shorthand. He *never* used text language before. Was he really that stressed out?

I'm at S Mission beach. I'm ok. There r a gazillon people around. Was about to head back.

Stay put. I'm on my way.

Plse don't be mad.

I'm not mad.

I shld hve waited 4 u 2 go 2 lunch with me.

It's okay. I'm not mad.

Promise? I can't deal with mad right now.

Shy, I'm not mad. I'm worried as hell. I just want to get to you.

Ok. Drive safe. I'm ok.

I'll be there as soon as I can.

Cheyenne took a deep breath. Just connecting with Faulkner via text was enough to make her feel a bit better. She looked down at her phone and contemplated listening to the message he'd left. Nope, she couldn't do it yet. She'd wait until she felt better. Stronger. She curled her arms around her drawn up legs again, her favorite position lately, and waited for Faulkner to come to her.

Chapter Thirteen

D UDE'S HANDS SHOOK as he drove toward South
Mission Beach. Cheyenne was right, it wasn't
secluded, there probably *were* a gazillion people around,
but he still worried about her. He'd been upset when
she hadn't called after her lunch should've been over,
but that only lasted about five minutes. It wasn't like
Cheyenne to let him worry or to not contact him.
Concern had taken over the anger quickly.

Obviously the lunch with her family hadn't gone
well. Dammit. Dude had a lot more experience in
dealing with disappointed parents than Cheyenne did.
He'd wanted to be there to be a buffer, to make sure
they didn't say anything cutting. His instincts had
obviously been right on. Something had happened.

Now Dude only wanted to get to Cheyenne and
comfort her. Whatever it took. He'd been so relieved
when Caroline had called him and told him she'd just
talked to Shy and that she was okay. She'd told him
briefly about how Shy had wanted to call him, but had

waited, then the longer she waited the more she thought he'd get angrier and angrier. The thought saddened Dude. It was obvious they needed to have a talk.

Cheyenne's need to please ran deep, but Dude didn't want her afraid to talk to him for any reason. And he certainly didn't want her to be scared of him, of how he'd react to anything she'd tell him.

After the longest thirty minutes of his life, Dude pulled into the parking lot at South Mission Beach. It wasn't as crowded as he'd seen it in the past, which he was thankful for. It meant he could easily find a place to park. He pulled out his phone and sent a quick text to Cheyenne.

I'm in the parking lot. Where are you?

Her answer came immediately.

left dwn the beach.

Dude pocketed his phone and started walking. He found Cheyenne not too far down from the parking lot. She was sitting forlornly in the sand, watching the ocean, not looking for his arrival.

Not bothering to take off his combat boots, Dude trekked out to where his woman sat sadly in the sand. He stopped behind her and eased himself to the sand. He bracketed her body with his, knees on either side of her, and wrapped his arms around her. He rested his head on her shoulder and waited.

Cheyenne felt cocooned in Faulkner's arms. He sat still and quiet behind her as he took her into his arms. She felt warm for the first time since she'd left the coffee shop that afternoon. She sighed. She needed this, she needed Faulkner.

"Hey," she said softly.

"Hey."

"I should've called. I'm sorry."

"It's okay, Shy."

"No, it's really not. I'm sorry if I worried you. I just…I thought you'd be mad. You asked me to call you and I didn't. Then it all just snowballed in my head. The longer I went without calling you, the madder I thought you'd get."

Her voice fell enough that Dude had to lean forward and turn his head to hear her.

"I don't like it when you're mad at me. Even though you haven't really even *been* mad at me yet, I can't stand the *thought* of you being mad at me. I think that's what it was. I want to make you happy."

"Shy…"

Cheyenne interrupted him. "And now, I've disappointed you. I don't know which is worse really. Fuck, I'm not like this. I'm not a wuss. The only thing I can say in my defense is that I've had a bad day."

Dude had enough of this. He scooted himself

around until he was sitting at Cheyenne's side. "Stop, Shy. I'm not mad and you didn't disappoint me. You worried me. There's a huge difference."

"I didn't mean to."

"I know. But we need to talk about this. We should've talked before now and that's on me. You aren't used to this. I love how we are. I love how you do what I tell you in our bed. I can't tell you what it means to me. I crave that. I need that. But outside the bedroom? No. I love the contradiction that is you. You're not afraid to call out my friends when they say dumb shit. You're brave enough to take on an entire police department when you have a bomb strapped to your chest. You're compassionate enough to allow assholes to strap said bomb to your chest, just so two other people don't have to go through that."

He kissed the top of her head and continued. "I'm going to get mad, Shy. I'm probably going to yell at some point. It doesn't mean I don't love you. Don't be afraid of me. Don't be scared to tell me to fuck off. If I overwhelm you, tell me. Remember when I told you we don't need safe words? It still holds, Shy. If you need me to back off, just say the word and I will."

"You love me?"

"Yes. I know it's soon, and crazy and I'm not even sure how it happened. I've waited for you my whole life. Not someone *like* you, but *you*. I know you don't have the experience to realize this, but what we have in the bedroom is unique. Unique and special. It's something I've never had with anyone else, ever. And it's not just about the sex. It's about who you are as a person. We've gotten to know each other over the last month and I *like* you Cheyenne." Dude's voice dropped. "I'm sorry your family disappointed you."

Cheyenne's eyes immediately filled with tears. "I should've known better, Faulkner. They've been like that my entire life. But when Karen told me she felt bad for those guys' families, I lost it. I couldn't believe she had more empathy for them than me. *Me*! Her flesh and blood. And Mom didn't say a word in my defense." After a beat Cheyenne said sadly, "I think I disowned them today."

"Good."

At Faulkner's heartfelt comment, Cheyenne peered up at him.

Dude repeated himself. "Good. You don't need that shit in your life. I'm your family now. Me and the guys. And of course their women."

He paused. As much as Dude wanted to demand she return the words to him, he moved on. She'd say them when she was ready.

"We have to talk about today a bit more, Shy."

"I won't do it again, I swear. I know I have this need to please you, but hearing you remind me it's okay to say no to you makes me feel better."

"Did you listen to the message I left you?"

Cheyenne was quiet for a moment. Then she shook her head.

Dude tsked at her. "Listen to it."

"I will."

"Now."

"I said I'd listen to it later, Faulkner."

"Give me your phone." Dude knew he was pushing it. Hell, he'd just told her that if he pushed her too hard or if she didn't want to do something all she had to do was let him know and he'd back off. But he couldn't back off of this.

Sighing, Cheyenne handed it over. She watched as Faulkner pushed some icons on the screen then turned the microphone toward them. He'd pushed play on the message and put it on speaker.

Cheyenne tensed. Oh shit, she didn't want to listen to what he had to say when Faulkner was right there...

Hey Shy. I'm worried about you. I'm sure something happened at lunch with your family. Will you please call or text me? If you need space, no problem, but I just need to know you're safe. Hope to hear from you soon.

The message ended and Cheyenne swallowed. "You weren't mad." Cheyenne looked up at the man sitting beside her. She'd been so afraid he'd yell at her, she'd totally underestimated him.

"No Shy, I wasn't mad. I told you, I was worried."

"I'm sorry."

"No more apologies. We're still learning about each other. We're still getting to know each other and figuring out the dynamics of our relationship. As I said, I'm sure there'll be times I'll be mad, just as there'll be times you'll be pissed at me. It's called a relationship, Shy. It's normal and healthy. If you need space, just let me know, I'll give it to you, but only if I know you're safe while you have it. Deal?"

"Deal. Thank you, Faulkner."

"You're welcome, Shy. Now, can we please go home?"

"Yeah. We can go home."

Dude stood up and held out his hand to Cheyenne. She grabbed it and he helped her stand up. His eyes glittered as he looked at her.

"What flavor today?" Dude leaned in and took her lips in a quick hard kiss. He ran his tongue over her lips as he pulled back. "Grape. Yum."

Cheyenne just shook her head at Faulkner and licked her lips, trying to get her equilibrium back.

Dude took her hand and towed her back to the parking lot. "As much as I'd like to refuse to let you drive, I think you'd probably get irritated with me if I demanded that, wouldn't you?"

Cheyenne simply nodded. "I'm okay to drive, Faulkner."

"Okay. I'll see you at home?"

"Yeah, home."

They smiled at each other and Dude gave her one last kiss before making sure she was buckled up in the seat. He shut the door behind her and turned around to head to his truck. He couldn't wait to show her how much she meant to him tonight. Cheyenne might not have said the words, but she showed him with her actions every day that he meant something to her. Dude would be patient. At least he'd *try* to be patient.

Chapter Fourteen

CHEYENNE GIGGLED AT Summer and Alabama. Caroline had called Cheyenne that morning and told her they were all going out. It was about a month after the horrendous lunch with her family and Cheyenne had blossomed under Faulkner's affection.

Their love life continued to be scorching hot and Cheyenne loved every second of it. There was something so freeing about being able to let go and have Faulkner make all the decisions. And it was something he excelled at. He knew exactly what to say and do to maximize her pleasure. Cheyenne knew she'd never get enough of him.

She hadn't yet told him she loved him. She had no idea why, just that she was waiting for the perfect time. Cheyenne wanted it to be romantic and meaningful. Saying it in the middle of sex didn't seem right, but right afterwards wasn't either. Faulkner wasn't the "go out to a fancy restaurant" type of guy, so that was out. So Cheyenne was struggling. She knew it was dumb, she should just say it, but so far she hadn't. The longer she waited the more the pressure to come up with the perfect time overwhelmed her.

Caroline had made it a point to include Cheyenne in their "girl's night out" festivities ever since Cheyenne had called her from the beach. The other women were hysterical. Cheyenne's respect for them had risen. She'd heard all of their stories over the last month at one time or another. Cheyenne couldn't believe what they'd all lived through, but when she'd tried to tell them that, they'd just laughed and said what *she'd* been through was just as impressive.

So now that Cheyenne had gotten over her nervousness, she loved hanging out with them. Sometimes she'd have lunch or dinner with just one of the girls, and other times it was all of them.

Cheyenne had slowly gotten to know the other guys on Faulkner's team as well. Caroline was right, on the outside they were all growly and gruff, but deep down, they *were* teddy bears.

It took an interaction between Hunter and Fiona for Cheyenne to finally "get" what Faulkner had tried to tell her that day on the beach.

Fiona and Cheyenne had gone out for lunch and made an impromptu decision to watch an afternoon movie. Not even thinking, they'd muted their phones and enjoyed the flick. After it was over Fiona looked at her phone and said, "Uh oh."

"What?"

"I was supposed to call Hunter after we were done with lunch so he could pick me up. He hasn't been able to get in touch with me, or you." She giggled. Actually giggled.

"Isn't he going to be pissed?"

Fiona had looked Cheyenne in the eye and said, "No. He'll be upset with me. He might yell, but I know deep down it's all stemmed in worry *for* me. There's a big difference between anger that is straight up anger, and anger that comes as a result of love."

It had clicked for Cheyenne. When Hunter had arrived at the theater to pick up Fiona, she watched as Hunter ranted and raved at Fiona. He'd lambasted her for being inconsiderate and selfish. Fiona had taken it in stride and apologized over and over. Hunter's anger blew itself out quickly and he took Fiona in his arms and held her tight.

It all made sense after seeing Hunter's reaction. Cheyenne hadn't brought it up with Faulkner yet, but she would. She knew he'd been extra careful lately not to upset her, and Cheyenne knew it had to stop. He was a SEAL, and more of a man than anyone she'd ever met. He had to let his feelings out. Cheyenne knew she had to convince Faulkner she wouldn't freak out if he did let them out on her now.

So tonight Caroline had called and informed her that they were all going out. Since Cheyenne wasn't working, she'd readily agreed.

Now they were sitting in *Aces*, their favorite bar, drinking amaretto and midori sours and doing the occasional shot. Summer and Alabama had challenged each other to see who could do a shot with no hands, drinking from the far side of the glass. It was obvious they'd fail, but it was hysterical to see them trying to strategize.

Cheyenne looked over at Mozart. He was sitting on the other side of the room pretending not to watch them. The guys had said the girls could go out all they wanted, as long as one of them was there to watch over them.

The guys pretended to be disgruntled about it, but Caroline had told her they all secretly loved it. She'd further informed Cheyenne that the girls only went out because of the incredible sex that followed when they arrived back home. She'd explained how their men loved doing them while they were drunk, so they encouraged the behavior by going out at least once a month.

Cheyenne giggled remembering how Caroline had told her about one episode with Matthew one month. She couldn't resist leaning in and whispering to Caroline that Faulkner had tied her up like that just last night. The look on Caroline's face was priceless. Cheyenne couldn't wait to see how Faulkner "did her drunk." If it was better than how he was giving it to her now, she was in serious trouble.

A pretty waitress, with short black hair and a tired look on her face, had been serving them. The other women seemed to know her as they called her by name, Jess, and joked with her as if she was one of the group.

Cheyenne told her friends that she felt bad that Jess kept walking back and forth from their table to the bar because she had a limp, and offered to go to the bar to get the drinks herself. The women had told her that it would embarrass Jess and not to worry about it. So Cheyenne had dropped it and after another shot or two stopped thinking of their waitress as handicapped, and instead as more of a savior from above who delivered drinks just as they needed them.

Cheyenne watched as Fiona counted to three and Summer and Alabama leaned over and grabbed the shot glass with their mouths and teeth. As they tried to grab the glass with their teeth and lean backward to try to down the shot, more liquid spilled down their chests than went into their mouths, soaking the front of each of their shirts in the process.

Laughing uncontrollably, Caroline, Fiona, and Cheyenne could only watch as the two women tried desperately to sop up the liquid before it ran all the way down their chests to their pants.

"So who won?" Summer asked with a crooked grin.

Cheyenne just shook her head. "You guys are such dorks. I think you both lost. Okay, let's go get you cleaned up." Cheyenne stepped between them and the three ladies made their way wobbling to the restroom at the bar. Stopping by Mozart, Summer kissed him long and hard. Sick of waiting, Alabama grabbed her arm and pulled.

"Come on, girl. You can do that later. It's girl's night out, not date night. You have to wait just like the rest of us have to."

Summer pulled herself out of her man's arms. Before continuing to the restroom, Summer leaned in and whispered something in his ear. Cheyenne watched as he smiled lazily and nodded, obviously pleased at whatever naughty thing Summer had told him.

The trio continued to the bathroom and they all piled inside. For a small bar, the restroom was surprisingly spacious. It was also very clean, which was one of the reasons the group always chose to come to *Aces*. There was nothing worse than having to pee while drunk in a filthy bathroom…at least that was what Caroline said.

Since Cheyenne hadn't ever tried to pee while drunk in a dirty bathroom, she couldn't argue one way or another, but she did appreciate not having to hover over a dirty toilet seat. It was much nicer to be able to sit on the seat, knowing it was clean.

"Boys are so lucky!" Cheyenne called out while relieving herself.

"What the hell are you babbling about, Cheyenne?" Alabama called out from the next stall over.

"Boys. They can stand up and pee. They don't have to worry about dirty bathrooms or filthy toilet seats."

"Lucky shits!" Summer screeched from the other side of Cheyenne.

The girls giggled and finished their business and were washing their hands, laughing about the trials and tribulations of women having to pee in public restrooms, when the door opened and a woman walked in. She had long brown hair and was wearing a pair of black jeans and a black long sleeved T-shirt.

"Hey!" she said cheerfully. Looking at Cheyenne she said, "I know you, you're that woman who was on the news a while back right? You were at that store when those men were shot weren't you?"

Cheyenne froze. She hadn't ever been recognized before, and there was something about the way the woman had asked about her, that sounded wrong.

Before she could affirm or deny the woman's words, Summer spoke up for her. "Hell yeah, she kicked *ass*! Those assholes didn't have a shot in hell at getting out of there. Our Cheyenne was too smart for them." She turned to Alabama and gave her a high five.

Cheyenne didn't take her eyes off the stranger. Her buzz was quickly fading. The woman didn't look happy. In fact she looked pissed.

"One of those assholes was my brother," she said in a low voice as she pulled out a pistol.

"Oh, Fuck," Alabama said quietly.

"Okay, look, I'm sorry, I didn't mean it." Summer tried to back pedal and apologize.

"Too late, bitch. You can't say something like that then in the next breath say you didn't mean it. You meant it. Just for that, you're coming with me too."

"Coming with you?"

"Yeah, we're all going for a ride."

Cheyenne tried to think fast. "Look, it's me you're pissed at...not them. They weren't there. I can tell you anything you want to know. I can tell you the last thing your brother said. Let them stay, just take me."

"Fuck that. The second we leave, they'll be on the phone calling in your military friends. No way in hell. You all have to come with me."

"How are you going to get us all to go with you?" Alabama asked steadily, as if she wasn't falling down drunk a minute ago.

The woman moved quickly and grabbed Summer's arm. She pulled her off balance and into her. The woman snagged her around the neck and tightened her hold, while also holding her pistol to the side of Summer's head. "If you don't come with me, I'll kill her. Right here in front of you. I'll blow her fucking brains out. What's it going to be?"

The woman was obviously stronger than she appeared, either that, or she was under the influence of some sort of drug. Summer struggled briefly, but wasn't able to break the woman's hold.

Cheyenne and Alabama watched helplessly as Summer struggled to breathe. It was an easy decision.

"Okay, we're coming. Don't hurt her. Please."

The woman eased up on Summer's throat a bit. "Don't try anything. I know one of your military friends is out there. We're going out the back door. Act normal or I'll fucking shoot her. I don't have anything to lose. After Hank was killed, my world went to shit anyway."

Cheyenne believed this woman would kill Summer if either of them made any wrong moves. Cheyenne's eyes filled with tears. Dammit. She didn't want to put her friends in danger. Summer had already been kidnapped once, she didn't need this. Cheyenne knew she had to get her new friends out of this somehow.

It wouldn't be long until Sam realized they'd been gone too long, especially with Summer being his. He'd come and look for them and when he couldn't find them, surely he'd know something was wrong.

Cheyenne and Alabama preceded the crazy woman

out of the restroom and toward the back door.

It was almost scary how easy it was for her to kidnap them right out of *Aces*. There was an SUV idling in the alley. A large man was sitting behind the wheel of the car and he glared at all of them as they exited the bar.

"What the hell, Alicia? I thought you were just going to get the store bitch? Who the hell are these other bitches?"

"I couldn't leave them all in there, Javier! Jesus! The second I left with her, the others would've been on the phone getting the military guys after us! Shit. Let's get the hell out of here."

Cheyenne tried one more time. "Please, don't take them, leave them here, they won't call anyone. I swear."

"Hell no, get in the car, bitch. Remember what I said. I'll kill your friends if you even *look* like you're planning something. I don't give a fuck about them, so you know I'm not lying."

"I'll do whatever you want. I promise. Just don't hurt them."

Cheyenne watched as an evil smile slid across Javier's face. "I see what you mean, Alicia. Good going. She'll be good as gold to keep her friends safe...won't you, sweetheart?"

Cheyenne swallowed the bile that crept up her throat. Shit. They were in serious trouble.

MOZART SHIFTED ON his seat. He couldn't wait to take Summer home and show her how much he loved "girls night out." She'd whispered in his ear that tonight was the night she was going to allow him to restrain her. They'd been working up to it. She still had nightmares about Ben Hurst and when she was restrained and helpless in his clutches. They both knew he wasn't Hurst, but sometimes the heart and the head differed in opinion.

He loved seeing the women drunk. They were cute and actually hilarious. Mozart only wished he could've filmed Summer and Alabama trying to down that shot without using their hands. Abe would've gotten a kick out of it.

The guys might bitch and moan to the women about having to babysit them, but the truth was, they all fought for the chance to watch over them each month. The women would laugh themselves silly if they saw the elaborate ritual they went through every month, each trying to outdo the other, for the chance to sit in a damn bar for a few hours watching the women tie one on. There were enough women now that it'd probably be a good idea to have two of them there when the ladies were getting drunk, just to be safe.

Mozart checked his watch. It'd been fifteen minutes since Summer and the others had passed him to go to the bathroom. He knew women tended to spend more time than men in the restroom, but fifteen minutes was pushing it. Gesturing at Caroline, who was also checking her watch, he gave a chin lift and motioned toward the bathroom.

Caroline leaned over to Fiona and told her she'd be right back. She passed Mozart and headed to the restroom. Mozart frowned when she returned before even a minute had passed.

"They aren't in there."

"Are you sure?"

"Sam, the bathroom only has three stalls, it's not like it's the size of a football stadium. There's no one in there."

They just looked at each other. Caroline reached for her phone. "They didn't text me."

Mozart pulled out his own phone. "Me either. Fuck."

They turned and almost ran into Jess, the waitress.

"Hey, Jess, have you seen Alabama, Summer, or Cheyenne? They went to the restroom about fifteen minutes ago and never came back."

Jess looked worried. "I'm sorry, I didn't see them at all. I was busy over there," Jess gestured toward the other side of the bar. "I was taking that large party's orders and then helping get the drinks ready."

Caroline and Mozart nodded and hurried back to the table. "Fiona, did any of the others text you by any chance?"

Sensing their urgency, Fiona checked her phone and shook her head after seeing she had no new texts.

Mozart didn't waste any more time. He dialed Wolf first.

"Hey, Mozart, ready to call it a night yet?"

"Summer, Alabama, and Cheyenne are MIA. They went to the restroom twenty minutes ago and disappeared. I haven't searched the premises yet, but wanted you to know."

"Caroline and Fiona?" Wolf's voice was clipped and businesslike.

"Right here with me."

"Put Ice on."

Mozart handed the phone to Caroline.

"Hey, Matthew."

"Ice, I need you and Fiona to stay close to Mozart. I'm calling the team, but until we know what the hell is going on I need you safe. Got me?"

"Of course, Matthew. I'll stay right here and won't let him out of my sight."

"Thank you, baby, please stay safe," Wolf said softly and with feeling before switching back to his no non-sense voice. "Put Mozart back on."

Caroline handed the phone back to Sam without a word.

"Yeah."

"Do a recon, then call Tex if you don't find them. He'll be able to track their phones. I'll call Dude and Abe and let them know. Call Benny and Cookie and tell them to meet you at *Aces*."

"Got it. Call if you find anything."

After hanging up with Mozart, Wolf clenched his fists momentarily before sighing and scrolling through his contacts. Neither Abe nor Dude were going to be happy to hear their women were missing.

CHEYENNE SAT IN the front seat of the SUV, huddled in misery. Alicia had crawled in the back seat with Summer and Alabama. She held the gun jammed into Alabama's side. Javier kept sneering at Cheyenne and winking at her viciously. It was seriously creeping Cheyenne out.

She tried to think through what was happening. So far, all she knew was that one of the men at the grocery store that day was Alicia's brother. She hadn't been able to figure out how Javier fit into everything yet.

The duo wasn't talking about where they were going or what was going to happen once they got there. The kidnapping was obviously pre-planned.

They drove for what seemed like hours, but was probably more like forty minutes or so, and pulled onto a dusty road. They bumped over the rough ground for at least a mile before coming to a stop outside a tiny house.

Alicia forced Alabama and Summer out, while Javier kept Cheyenne from exiting by latching tightly onto her arm and not letting go.

"Where is she taking them?" Cheyenne shrieked. "Let me go. "No, don't take them. Shit. No." She struggled against Javier's hold until he finally took his fist and rammed it into the side of her face.

"Shut the fuck up. Damn. Seriously."

Cheyenne shook her head. Her ears were ringing and she groaned. Shit that hurt. She tried a different tactic. "Look, if it's money you want, I can get it for you. I've got twenty thousand dollars in the bank, it's yours if you just let my friends go. They didn't do anything, they have nothing to do with this. Please don't hurt them, just take me and we'll go and get the money."

Javier didn't answer, but instead rolled down the passenger window and yelled, "Hurry the fuck up, Alicia, we ain't got time for this shit!"

"Keep your pants on, Javier. Fuck! I'm gettin' there!"

Before Javier could roll the window up again, Cheyenne yelled out the open window to her friends. "Hang in there you guys! I'm sure the guys are coming!"

"Your fucking Navy SEALS aren't coming, bitch." Javier growled at her.

Cheyenne was sick of this. "They *are*. They'll find you guys and shoot you down just like the snipers did to Alicia's brother!"

"If they come, they'll die."

Cheyenne stared at Javier, trying to decide if he was talking smack or if he was serious.

"We wired the entire place."

At the look of horror on Cheyenne's face, Javier laughed. "Poor, poor, Cheyenne. Not only will you lose your friends, but you'll also lose your precious SEAL. We've got cameras hooked up so we can watch too."

"But I thought you didn't know my friends would be here with me."

"Of course we did. We put on a show that you fucking bought hook, line, and sinker. Do you think we don't know that bitches can't pee by themselves? We figured you'd be with at least one of your friends. Having two? That'll just keep your SEALs occupied that much longer."

"No, Jesus, no."

"Yes, Jesus, yes." Javier mocked.

"Who are you? Why are you doing this?" Cheyenne asked desperately trying to figure out a way out of the horrible situation she found herself and her new friends in.

"Because one of those assholes was *my* brother too. Alicia and I met while filming a segment for one of the news shows. We watched you, hung out in the parking lot where you work. Memorized your schedule. We decided to band together to get revenge. Revenge is always sweeter when shared, don't you think?"

Cheyenne sobbed once, then choked it back. She flinched when she heard a gunshot ring out into the countryside. "Summer? Alabama?" she cried out frantically.

"We're okay!"

Cheyenne sighed in relief, then heard another gun shot. "Stop fucking shooting at my friends!" she screeched, hoping Alicia could hear her. Javier just laughed next to her, obviously not concerned about Alicia in the slightest. He rolled the window up, so Cheyenne couldn't hear what was happening in the little cabin anymore.

Cheyenne watched as Alicia exited the cabin. She didn't come straight to the car though. Cheyenne observed as she took wire and circled the cabin twice, making sure to twist the wires together as she went.

"She's setting the wires for the bomb," Javier told her, sounding as if he was telling her the weather forecast for the day. "The cabin is rigged to blow. There are trip wires all over the place. All it will take is one wrong step by your precious SEALs and your friends will be blown to bits right in front of their eyes."

"No," Cheyenne breathed. "Please, leave them

alone."

"Sorry, sweets. Too fucking late for that."

Cheyenne thought she was hyperventilating. Had Alicia shot Summer or Alabama? Were they inside the cabin dying right now?

Alicia came running back toward the SUV. She tore open the back door and was laughing as she plopped her butt on the seat and slammed the door behind her. "All set. The first shot scared them, but the second one shut the blonde up."

"No! What did you do?" Cheyenne tried to turn in her seat to she could leap over and hurt Alicia, but Javier just laughed and twisted the arm he still had in his grasp cruelly.

Cheyenne contorted her body to try to take the pressure off her arm as Javier twisted it in his grasp. He kept on twisting until Cheyenne heard a *pop*. The most incredible pain she could ever imagine swept over her, almost making her pass out. "Aahhhhhhh."

Cheyenne heard Javier and Alicia laughing through her pain.

"Did you break it?"

"Nah, just pulled it out of socket. That should keep her docile."

Cheyenne concentrated on not throwing up all over herself, the car, and Javier. She had no idea how she'd get out of this. How her friends would get out of it. She didn't even know if Summer was still alive. If Alicia had shot her, how long did she have before she had to see a doctor or she'd die? Cheyenne moaned. They were all in big trouble.

Chapter Fifteen

WOLF, ABE, MOZART, DUDE, AND BENNY surrounded an alley in the heart of the city. Cookie was back at *Aces* with Ice and Fiona, guarding them, waiting for intel from the team.

Wolf and Abe approached from the south while the other three SEALS approached from the north. Tex had traced the women's cell phones to this location. There was a large dumpster up against the wall and the men could hear sounds coming from inside it.

Cautiously and soundlessly the men approached. They had no idea what they would find inside, but all five men were fully concentrated on the dumpster. Wolf covered the south while Benny covered the north entrance. Mozart cautiously approached the dumpster, brought his flashlight up and without making a sound, lifted the lid.

After he peered inside, he lowered the lid and closed the dumpster carefully, then quickly backed away.

"Bomb," he said tonelessly.

The five men wasted no time retreating until they were standing at the end of the alley.

Mozart told his friends what he'd seen.

"All three cell phones are in there, strapped to a small bomb. I don't think it can do much damage, but we need to call it in."

"Do I need to go and check it out?" Dude asked, knowing he'd be able to tell with a glance how dangerous the bomb was.

"No, it's obvious they ditched the phones and they're just fucking with us," Abe commented with disgust.

"Fuck. I'll call Tex back and tell him to keep looking," Benny said, pulling out his phone and punching buttons while he said it.

"What the fuck is going on?" Dude growled out to no one in particular.

"This has to be connected to whatever happened in that grocery store. The bomb is just too much of a coincidence," Wolf theorized as the team stalked down the street back to Wolf's SUV. "Call Cookie, have him talk to Ice and Fiona again, see if he can't get *any* more information. Anything would help us at this point."

"They are never fucking going out again without us there, not even to pee." Dude was at the end of his rope. This was worse than the day Cheyenne had lunch with her family. At least then he knew she'd just had a bad day and was laying low. This? Some fucker had her who was smart enough to ditch their cells *and* create a hell of a diversion with them.

Benny piped up as they got to the SUV. "Tex is calling the cops to let them know about the explosive in the dumpster. He's as pissed as we are. He's seeing what he can find on surveillance tapes, although *Aces* doesn't really have good coverage. Since they had three women, they had to have had a bigger type car."

"Why do you think they all went? I mean if they were kidnapped by one person, it would've been hard to overpower them all," Benny further mused.

"Threats. He had to have threatened one of them. You know our women," Abe said in a low pissed off voice. "All he had to do was threaten to kill or hurt one of them and the others would've done whatever he said without a fight."

Out of the blue, Mozart turned away from the vehicle and stalked over to the nearest building and punched the wall. Blood immediately flowed from the broken flesh on his knuckles. Wolf and Benny went to him and put their hands on his arms, ready to restrain him if he went to punch the wall again.

Instead, Mozart put both hands against the wall and leaned heavily on it, head down. "Summer can't go through this again," he said in a low tortured voice. "She'll break. If she's fucking broken when I find her, someone's gonna die."

"We'll find her, Mozart," Wolf told his friend earnestly.

"Yeah? When? After she's been violated? After she's been tortured again? Seriously, you *know* what happened with Hurst last time. She can't go through this again."

"I know, Mozart. I know. Tex will find them. You know he can find anyone."

"He fucking better."

No one said a word for a moment. Thoughts about what the three women were going through flitted through each man's head. Finally Mozart pushed off the wall and walked up to Dude and Abe.

"I'm so fucking sorry you guys have to experience this. I'd hoped I'd be the only one to have to know what it feels like to have my woman stolen from me. I don't know who or what we're up against, but we have to get them back. Yesterday."

"We will, Mozart. We fucking will," Abe told him.

Dude didn't say a word. Hatred was burning in the back of his eyes. It was bad enough his friends' women were taken. But no one took *his* woman away from him. Cheyenne was his. He felt like a dog with a bone. Shy had said it straight out. She was his.

Dude *loved* Shy. It was all suddenly clear to him now. He didn't get it before. Oh he knew he had feelings for Cheyenne and he'd thought he'd loved her, had even told her so, but he hadn't understood how his teammates could put everything they'd ever known aside for a woman. But now? He fucking got it. When Fiona had run because of flashbacks and Cookie was out of the country? When Abe realized how badly he'd hurt Alabama and how much his words had shredded her? When Summer had been taken and Mozart had been frantic to find her? Even when they were in the middle of the ocean and Wolf had stepped aside and let someone else run the mission to rescue Ice...Dude finally understood.

Love. His friends loved their women with all they had, just as Dude loved Cheyenne. She was his. It didn't matter that this was the twenty first century and women didn't "belong" to anyone anymore. It didn't matter that Cheyenne was independent and could function perfectly fine on her own without him.

Deep down, some basic instinct they had, insisted that the women were theirs. Theirs to protect, to feed, to clothe, to love. Theirs. Cheyenne was *his,* dammit. He needed her in his life, in his house, in his bed. Hell, he just needed her around. To see her smile, to see her chew on her damn thumbnail. To love. That's what love was. It wasn't simple affection, it wasn't enjoying her company. It was all consuming and in the very marrow of his bones.

"Let's go," was all Dude could get out between his clenched teeth. He was on edge. He knew Mozart and Abe were feeling the same way. Their women were in danger. This was probably the most important mission they'd ever been on. The team was already close, but now, they were functioning as one. Wolf knew it could've easily been Caroline. It was pure chance that it hadn't been.

The men climbed back into the SUV without a word. This shit had to end. Whatever this shit was, it totally had to end.

TWO HOURS LATER, the entire team convened around a small cabin about twenty miles outside the city. Caroline and Fiona had gone back to Caroline's house and were accompanied by three SEALs from another team on the base. Wolf wasn't putting their safety to chance. The women had accepted the protection without a word, which pissed all the men off because it meant the women were feeling vulnerable and freaked by everything that had happened. Usually Ice would've flipped out on Wolf and argued against having any strangers in their house, but she'd just kissed him, hugged him hard, and told him to bring her friends home.

Tex had come through again. Just when the men thought there was no way Tex would be able to help them this time, he figured it out. The man could find a damn needle in a haystack, from a thousand miles away.

He'd used some sort of math/physics/engineering algorithm to study the traffic patterns, along with cell phone usage and surveillance cameras to pinpoint the exact damn vehicle the women had been taken in. Once he'd found the car, it was a simple matter, Tex's words, to hack into the government's satellites and track it.

Everyone on the team knew what Tex was doing was illegal, but no one said a word. If it helped get their women back, no one gave a fuck.

Tex had been able to track the car to this shitty little cabin. It was eerily quiet. Too quiet. Something was definitely not right. Dude wanted to yell out Cheyenne's name, to see if she was okay, to see if she was even in the damn building, but he wouldn't. This mission was on communication lockdown. If the kidnapper was in there, they wanted to surprise him.

Dude led the way to the cabin, every few steps he scanned the area, looking for…something. He wasn't sure what. The hair on the back of his neck was sticking straight up. This wasn't right. He signaled for everyone to hold up.

Everyone stopped immediately and waited for Dude. Taking his eyes off the ground, Dude looked around. He willed his brain to see what his eyes weren't. Finally he stopped and turned his head back to where he was just looking. There.

"Fucking camera in the tree," he tonelessly said to his teammates through his mic.

After a moment Wolf said, "There's one over here too."

"Here too," Abe chimed in.

"Wolf, the bastards are watching us," Dude commented unnecessarily.

"But are they watching from inside the cabin or from elsewhere?" Benny chimed in, asking what everyone else had been thinking.

Without waiting for Wolf to approve of his actions, Dude yelled out. His voice carried across the clearing to the house. "Shy? Summer? Alabama?"

The men waited. Hoping.

"Here! We're here!"

"Thank fuck!" Abe breathed, recognizing Alabama's voice.

"Don't come in!" Alabama continued to yell from inside the cabin. "The bastards have rigged the entire place with some sort of explosive!"

Every man froze in place. Dude looked around, now that he knew what he was looking for, it was easy to see. The wires around the cabin weren't hidden all that well. He'd been so concerned about looking for hidden trip wires, he'd missed the obvious ones right in front of him. The kidnapper had obviously thought he was being sneaky by placing some wires around the cabin in the path, hoping the SEALs would step on them and set off the bomb. Idiots.

"Is Summer in there with you? Cheyenne?" Mozart called out.

"Summer is. They took Cheyenne though."

"They? Jesus, how many people are involved in this?" Cookie muttered through the mic.

"Okay, sit tight, sweetheart. Anyone else around?" Everyone could tell Abe wanted nothing more than to rush into the cabin and see for himself that Alabama was all right, but he was too well-trained to do anything to fuck up the mission, especially when explosives were involved.

"No, it's just us in here. But, Summer's hurt."

With Alabama's words, the anxiety level of the men suddenly shot up. Dude blocked out the fact that Cheyenne wasn't in the cabin and got to work trying to piece together how the explosives were set up and how to disarm them. The faster he figured it out, the faster they could get to Summer and Alabama, and the faster he could find Shy.

"Benny, you and Cookie work on dismantling the cameras. Be careful, the bastards might have rigged those too. Leave one up and running. I'll call Tex and give him a head's up on the cameras, he might be able to backtrack the signal and find the fucking nest. They have to be watching us for a reason. Let's use their voyeurism against them. Fucking assholes."

CHEYENNE COULDN'T BELIEVE this was happening to her again. Once again she was covered in miles of duct tape. Her shoulder was screaming at her. Javier really *had* pulled it out of its socket when he'd wrenched it in the car. She supposed the tape holding her still was probably helping her keep it immobile, but it still hurt like nothing Cheyenne had experienced before.

The duo had driven her back into the city and to an apartment building. They'd broken in through a door in a back alley and dragged her down the stairs to the basement where they'd begun the process of taping her up.

Javier and Alicia had cackled the entire time they'd wrapped her in tape. Unlike in the grocery store though, they'd wrapped three bombs up this time. Then Alicia thought it'd be funny to wrap the tape around her neck and head too. Luckily Javier had stopped her before she could cover her mouth and nose with the stuff too.

So now Cheyenne was literally mummified. She couldn't move. She was lying on the floor, ankles, legs, body, arms, head, all taped up. Cheyenne almost laughed thinking about how much all the tape must have cost.

She couldn't help herself. She couldn't run, she couldn't get out of the way, she could only lay on the ground and watch Javier and Alicia. Cheyenne closed her eyes, she'd had enough of watching them. Apparently being horrible human beings in the middle of a kidnapping made them horny. They'd had sex on the floor right next to her. Since she'd been mummified she couldn't move, she couldn't do anything but close her eyes and wish like hell Faulkner was there.

After getting off, Javier pulled out a hand-held device and hunkered over it with Alicia, the two of them cackling with glee and laughing manically. It was the video feed of the cabin. They were watching as the SEALs made their way to the cabin.

"I wish this had sound!" Alicia complained. "But it's fucking great. Look at them, all in stealth mode. I can understand what you see in them, they're hunky and hot...too bad they're all going to get blown up...along with your stupid friends."

Cheyenne struggled on the floor. No! Dammit no! She stopped struggling when all it did was make her shoulder hurt more. She wasn't going anywhere. She had to believe the guys knew what they were doing. They weren't going to just barge in to the cabin without being cautious. Dude would see the explosives. He had to.

"What the fuck are they doing? Why aren't they going in? You said they would rush right up to the door and bust in!" Javier complained to Alicia.

"Well, I figured they would. We had two of their women. They're hotheaded military guys! That's what they're supposed to do!"

"Well, they're not! Look! That one guy sees the camera! Fuck!"

The two were quiet a moment as they watched the action play out on the little black and white handheld device. After another few minutes, Javier sighed in exasperation.

"We gotta get out of here. Obviously they're gonna get the girls out. Fuck this."

"What about her?" Alicia whined.

"That part of the plan doesn't change. In about eight hours she's gonna blow up, so who the fuck cares."

"But she knows who we are…"

Javier growled and got in Alicia's face. "Yeah, and so do those bitches that are about to be rescued. You think they aren't gonna tell those SEALs who we are? Huh?"

"But we can't just leave *her* here…she's going to tell them we're headed to Mexico."

"In about eight hours she's gonna be dead so who. the. fuck. cares."

"All right, all right, jeez. Keep your pants on. Shit. Should we change the timing so that thing goes off sooner?"

"Too late, dumbass. We already covered it all up with the tape," Javier said impatiently. "Leave the TV here with her. We don't want to have it with us in case they can somehow trace it back. Besides, she can watch her friends either get rescued, or blown to bits. Seems fair to me."

Cheyenne watched as Alicia threw her head back and cackled at Javier's suggestion. She then came over to where Cheyenne lay helpless on the floor, and propped the little device up next to her head with a box.

"There you go, bitch. I hope they all get blown to pieces. You can watch and then wait for your own bombs to go off and blow *you* to pieces."

"You're a piece of shit," Cheyenne croaked out.

"No, you got my brother killed and you got Javier's brother killed. *You're* the piece of shit."

Cheyenne could only watch as the two kidnappers gathered up their stuff and left without a backward glance. She looked around, knowing that if the bombs did go off she'd die, but probably more importantly, so would a lot of other people.

She was underneath an apartment complex. People *lived* there. If the bombs went off it would surely do some damage to the building itself. It might even collapse. If it did, no one would even find her body…if there was anything left to find. Cheyenne suppressed a sob. She couldn't cry. There was nothing worse than snot running down your face when you couldn't wipe it away. There was still time though. Eight hours. Maybe Faulkner could find her in time.

She turned her attention to the little television screen propped next to her. Cheyenne could barely make out the cabin, but she saw the SEALs walking around it and leaning over. Hopefully they were able to make it safe enough to get Summer and Alabama out. Hopefully Summer wasn't dead. She could only watch as the best people she'd ever met, worked frantically to rescue her friends.

Cheyenne drank in the sight of Faulkner. She'd know him anywhere. She'd spent weeks memorizing every inch of his body, at his command. She knew the placement of every scar, every mole, every nook and cranny. Cheyenne had no idea if she'd ever see him in person again, or be able to feel his body against hers, so watching Faulkner move around the small cabin, she memorized everything about him all over again.

DUDE STOOD OFF to the side and observed Abe holding Alabama and Mozart comforting Summer as Cookie made sure she was stable enough to be transported down to the city. Summer had been shot, but luckily the bullet had only grazed her upper arm. Alabama had immediately done some basic first aid and stopped the bleeding. She'd be okay.

Dude was relieved both women were all right, but the burning in his gut wouldn't stop. Where the hell was Cheyenne? What was *she* going through? He stood back from the others, fists clenched, wanting to do something, but not sure what it was they could do yet.

Remembering the cameras in the trees, he looked up at the one they hadn't taken down yet. Tex was working on tracing the feed. Were the bastards watching them now? He kept his eyes on the camera, it was easier than watching his friends holding their women.

CHEYENNE DIDN'T KNOW how much time had passed since Alicia and Javier had left. She'd kept her eyes on the blurry little black and white screen in front of her. The angle wasn't great, but she could still make out when the group went into the cabin and when both Summer and Alabama came out.

Her heart about stopped when she saw Summer being carried by Sam, but relaxed a bit when she saw she was moving and holding on to her man of her own accord.

Even though it was torturous to see her friends so close, but so far away, she kept watching. After a moment she noticed Faulkner. He was standing off to the side, not interacting with his friends in any way. He was looking up at her…well up at the camera. Cheyenne could imagine she saw the tick in his jaw. They knew the cameras were there. They *knew*.

A single tear fell from Cheyenne's eye before she brutally swallowed them down. If they knew about the cameras then they had some plan. She had to believe that. Cheyenne had no idea how they were going to get her out of *this*, but if anyone could, her SEALs could.

Cheyenne continued to watch until the group finally moved out of camera range. They were obviously leaving. The feed continued to play but all Cheyenne could see were the trees gently blowing in the wind and the cabin sitting forlornly in the clearing.

She hoped with all her being that she hadn't just seen the last of her friends…and of Faulkner.

"COME ON, LET'S go. We have to get Summer to the hospital," Wolf ordered, heading back for the SUV.

Dude finally took his gaze off the camera and looked at his teammates. Wolf was looking at him with concern. Benny and Cookie just looked pissed and Mozart and Abe looked relieved to have their women back, but they also looked determined.

"No one fucks with this team. And no one fucks with our women and gets away with it," Abe said with feeling. "We're not stopping until we find her, Dude."

"The woman's name was Alicia and she called the guy Javier," Alabama said suddenly. "They said some of the guys in the grocery store that day were their brothers."

With those two sentences, it finally all made sense.

"Revenge," Cookie said, stating the obvious.

"Obviously making bombs and being an asshole runs in the family," Summer quipped from Mozart's arms.

No one laughed, but everyone appreciated her attempt at levity.

"We can't leave yet. What if Cheyenne is up here somewhere? We'll lose too much time if we all head back to the city and then have to come back up here once Tex traces that feed."

Benny was being practical, and it sucked. He was right. Dude didn't know whether to continue to search the woods nearby, or to head back down to the city. He closed his eyes and bowed his head, thinking.

Okay, so these were siblings to the guys killed. They wanted revenge. Would they want to stash Cheyenne up in the woods where they could torture her, or would they bring her back into civilization for some reason?

Dude raised his head, knowing deep in his gut his conclusion was right. "They're in the city."

Without asking how Dude was so sure, the men strode toward the car.

Alabama wasn't so sure. "But Dude, they brought us

up here, why wouldn't they have stashed Cheyenne somewhere up here too?"

Not slowing down, Dude tried to explain. "They want revenge. You guys were a diversion. They wanted us to waste time up here. They took her back down to where there are people. They want to hurt Cheyenne, yes, but they also want to hurt us. They know what we do, killing as many people as possible is their goal. They want to show that SEALs aren't perfect, that we can't always rescue people as I did that day in the grocery store."

"But that's crazy," Alabama whispered.

"Yeah," Dude agreed, but said no more.

It was a tight fit in the SUV, but no one complained. Their mission wasn't done. Cheyenne was still out there…somewhere.

Chapter Sixteen

SEVEN MEN STOOD around a table on the Naval base. The team's CO, Commander Hurt, had joined them and was listening to the information Tex was giving them.

"The camera feed definitely leads back into the city. Because of all the buildings and interference, it's hard to pinpoint exactly where."

"Try." Dude's voice was strained. It was obvious he was hanging on by the merest thread.

"I am, Dude. I swear to Christ, I am. Have the police had any luck in breaking Alicia and Javier yet?"

Wolf had contacted the commander and he in turn had contacted the police as soon as they'd left the cabin. He'd explained who the people were that kidnapped Summer and Alabama. Both women had said they were more than willing to press charges.

Javier and Alicia were dumb enough to still be in their apartments packing to flee out of the country. They'd been taken into custody without trouble, but were refusing to say anything about Cheyenne. They denied having anything to do with the kidnappings and denied even knowing who Cheyenne was.

Wolf answered Tex, "No, they aren't saying anything. Alicia let something slip though, and it might be nothing, but she said she might be willing to talk in the morning. We don't know why the morning will make a difference though."

"It's another bomb," Dude said into the silence that followed Wolf's statement. "It's the only thing that makes sense. They've stashed her somewhere and immobilized her with a bomb, just as their brothers did in the store. She'll talk in the morning because it'll be too late then. The bomb will have gone off."

Surprisingly, it was the commander who lost it. "God *damn* it! Get me the fucking Police Chief on the phone *now*!"

No one was really sure who Commander Hurt was talking to, but Tex apparently decided he was talking to him. "Connecting now, Sir…Ringing…you're on."

"Yeah?" A voice barked out from the speaker sitting on the table in the room.

"Chief? Listen, this is Commander Hurt. There's been a development in the case…"

The Commander proceeded to explain their suspicions to the Police Chief and why time was of the essence. The Chief agreed to put more pressure on

Alicia and see if they couldn't get her to tell them where they'd stashed Cheyenne.

"Tex…"

"I know, I know, I'm working on it."

"We're running out of time," Dude's voice finally cracked. He could sense it was almost too late. He knew he'd need every second he could get to try to get Cheyenne out of whatever fucked up situation the two yahoos had put her in. *This* was what his entire SEAL career had prepared him for. *This* was why he was a natural with explosives. To save this woman's life. To save his woman's life.

"Dude, I swear to God I'm going to find her. Those schmucks aren't very fucking smart, they sure as hell aren't smarter than me. Mother fuckers." Tex's rant stopped abruptly. "Wait…oh fucking hell. Are you shitting me?"

"What? Jesus Tex. What?"

Every man in the room turned their complete attention on the innocuous looking phone sitting on the table.

"Okay, I'm not one hundred percent sure, but I don't want to wait to *be* completely sure. I've narrowed the feed down to a city block. There are three buildings. An office building, an apartment building and what looks from the satellite photos to be an abandoned old factory. I think there are plans to turn it into some fancy-ass duplexes or something."

Wolf turned to Dude. "Which one?" He had complete confidence that Dude would know.

Dude closed his eyes to think. He couldn't be wrong about this. Yes, all the buildings were close together, but for all the people involved, for Cheyenne, he couldn't be wrong. He worked through the situation out loud.

"Okay, the abandoned building is out. That wouldn't cause enough damage. They wanted people hurt or killed. They want to make a statement. Both of the other buildings have people in them. Tex," Dude's eyes opened and he began to pace, "tell me about the layouts of each."

They could hear Tex clicking on his computer keys. "The office building is a four story building which houses seventeen different organizations. They're split over the four different floors. Elevators in the NW corner as well as in the middle. Stairways in the SW and NE corners. The apartment building is also four stories high. There are twenty apartments on each floor for a total of eighty apartments. Seventy five of the apartments are currently occupied. There are two vacant apartments on the second floor, one on the third and two on the fourth. There are three elevators in the lobby and two stairwells. Both are emergency stairwells with exits to the street."

"Entrances?" Dude barked, still pacing.

"The offices have two emergency exits leading out to the street from the stairwells. There are two main entrances into the building and there seems to be a security desk in the lobby checking employee IDs and accepting packages. The apartment building also has two entrances, both are swipe card access, but no security desk in the lobby. There's a mail room on the first floor, accessible to the general public, but there's a swipe card door that leads from the mailroom into the lobby."

"Basements? Access to them?"

"Both buildings have basements, negative on the access for the office, but both stairwells in the apartment access both the basement and the roof."

Dude was heading for the door to the conference room before Tex had finished speaking. "She's in the basement of the apartment building," he said as he reached the door.

No one asked how Dude knew, no one questioned him. It was uncanny how Dude could figure things out sometimes. If he said Cheyenne was in the basement of the apartment building, she was in the basement of the apartment building.

The commander was barking into the phone at Tex. "I'll notify the Police and Fire Chiefs…set off the alarms remotely Tex, clear both those buildings and get people out of the area. I don't know how much time we have, but we have to get everyone out."

Dude was focused on Cheyenne. The commander was right, he didn't know how much time he had, but in his gut he was afraid it wasn't going to be enough.

CHEYENNE HEARD THE alarms in the building above her pealing. She had no idea what time it was or how much of the eight hours had passed since Alicia and Javier had left. Her shoulder didn't hurt anymore, she figured it was because it was numb. She knew when a shoulder was pulled out of its socket it was a matter of time before blood flow was stopped.

Her eyes went back to the black and white screen. She couldn't take her eyes from it. It was the last place she'd seen Faulkner and she needed to hold that memory in her head.

Cheyenne hoped like hell the sounds of the fire alarm above her head meant the building was being cleared. She couldn't think that it was because of her. She wouldn't get that hope built up inside her, only to have it dashed.

The trees swaying at the cabin on the screen mesmerized her. The door to the cabin was open and every now and then would slowly creep shut, then be blown open again a couple of minutes later. She kept her attention on the little screen. It was better than thinking about her own situation, or about how many people might die because of her.

DUDE WAS COMPLETELY focused on the building in front of him. His Shy was there, he could instinctively feel it. The set up was perfect. The stairwell door in the alley had been propped open with a small rock in the doorjamb. The door wasn't able to latch because of the small obstruction. It was where Alicia and Javier had to have entered.

Dude turned to Benny and Cookie. "I'm going down there alone."

"No you aren't," Benny immediately returned.

"Look, we all know what we're going to find down there and I'm the only one who can get her out of it."

"No, you aren't, Dude," Cookie argued. "We're a team, and you're wasting fucking time. Wolf has it under control up here. We're going down there with you and we'll figure out how to save her. Now shut the hell up and move your ass."

Cookie was right. They didn't have any time to spare. Dude turned on his heel and headed down the stairs. The three men turned the corner and stopped dead. Dude had been right. Cheyenne was there, but she was in deep trouble. They all were.

Cheyenne thought she heard something, but didn't

bother to turn her head away from the screen. She wanted to stay in the moment, to remember watching as her friends were saved. Suddenly she felt a hand on her cheek. No, she felt *Faulkner's* hand on her cheek. She'd recognize that scarred and rough touch anywhere. Was she dreaming?

"Shy, I'm here."

Cheyenne forced her eyes away from the screen and looked up. It *was* Faulkner. And Hunter. And Kason. Oh shit.

"No. Just go, seriously. Please. Just go."

"We've been here before, Shy. Just let me help you. I'll get you out of this."

"No, Faulkner, you can't. This isn't like last time."

"The hell it isn't. I'm not letting you go, Shy. You're mine. You said it. I take care of what's mine. Remember?"

Cheyenne couldn't hold back the sob. She looked over at Kason and Hunter and whispered, "Please, he can't this time, take him and go."

"Fuck no, Cheyenne, he's not leaving and neither are we," Cookie said harshly, his eyes roving over her body, trying to come up with a plan of action.

"Cheyenne, the others are evacuating the building. They're getting everyone out and away. We'll just get this shit off you and Dude will take care of whatever's underneath and we'll get you out too."

Bizarrely, Cheyenne didn't react to this statement, she simply turned back to Faulkner and asked in a weirdly monotone voice, "How long has it been since you rescued Summer and Alabama?"

Dude looked down at his watch, then back into Cheyenne's eyes. "About six hours."

"They said eight hours. It's probably been about seven by now. There's no way you can figure all this out in an hour."

"Bullshit, Shy. An hour's a piece of cake. Hell, I thought I'd only have minutes. Trust me."

"I do, Faulkner, I do, but…"

"No. No buts. You do or you don't. Period, Shy."

Cheyenne looked deep into Faulkner's eyes. She tried not to think about being blown to bits, to think about *him* being blown to bits right next to her. He hadn't asked for much from her, only her submission and along with that her trust. She trusted him to take care of her sexually, she trusted that he'd never willingly hurt her, she had to trust him here too. This was what he did.

"I trust you and I love you."

Cheyenne watched as Faulkner closed his eyes briefly. When he opened them again, there was determination shining in them. He pressed his lips together then told her, "When I get you home, you're going to pay for waiting until *now* to give me the words,

Shy."

When she opened her mouth, he waved her off, completely focused on what he had to do again. "Tell me what's under this tape. Tell me everything you can."

"There are three bombs as far as I know. One between my knees, one at my belly, and one on my chest. They were ticking before they strapped them to me. I can't feel my arm, Javier dislocated my shoulder before they taped me up."

Blocking out her comment about her shoulder for a moment, Dude asked, "Which one did they wrap up first? And can you breathe all right? Anything else wrong I need to know about before I start?"

"They started with my feet. I couldn't kick them if they were taped together. They immobilized me and started from my feet and worked their way up. And yes, I can breathe okay." Cheyenne paused a moment then said softly, "I'm scared, Faulkner."

"Me too, Shy, me too," Faulkner said unexpectedly, "But I swear, I'm getting you out of this."

"I know you are. Don't worry about hurting me. I can take it. Do whatever you need to in order to get the tape off and these damn bombs disarmed."

"There's no need for you to hurt, Cheyenne," Cookie said, pulling something out of his pack. "Dude, I have some morphine here."

"Do it," Dude didn't even hesitate. He knew he was

going to have to hurt Shy, and he wanted to make sure he kept it to a minimum.

"Oh fuck, Faulkner, you know what those kinds of drugs do to me."

Dude smiled for the first time in hours. He quickly leaned down and kissed Shy's duct taped forehead and looked her in the eyes. "I don't give a fuck what comes out of your mouth, baby, as long as you're alive and breathing."

"Cheyenne, I'm going to have to inject this into your thigh. I can't see exactly where it's going in, so I apologize in advance for causing you any pain."

"Hunter, it's gonna hurt a lot more to be blown to pieces, so I don't give a fuck about where you stick me, just shut up and do it already."

Benny chuckled at the crankiness of her voice as Cookie quickly inserted the needle through the duct tape around her thigh.

Still looking into Faulkner's eyes, Cheyenne told him, "Don't wait, get it done."

As much as he wanted to wait until the morphine took effect, Cheyenne was right, Dude didn't have the luxury of waiting.

"Benny, come up here to her head, don't touch the tape around her head that can come off later. Start on her chest. Be extremely careful. Don't touch the device at all. Loosen up what you can. Cookie, do the same starting at her hips. I'm going to start down here. Remove only what's necessary to get to the devices, nothing else."

The three men got to work.

Dude pulled out his K-bar knife, as the others did the same, and sliced at the tape around Cheyenne's ankles. He had to actually saw through the material because there was so much of it. Alicia and Javier had spent some time wrapping her. They hadn't wanted her to be able to get out of there easily. Hell, they hadn't wanted her to get out at all.

At last Dude freed her ankles. Once they were separated it was easier for him to cut through the tape holding her legs together.

He finally got to the explosive device between her knees. He took precious time to free as much tape from above and below the device as he could.

"Faulkner, the last time you were between my legs like this, you ordered me not to come, I don't think that'll be an issue right now."

Dude couldn't help but smile. Jesus, he couldn't believe how the filter of Cheyenne's words turned itself off when she had some drugs in her system. "Shy..." he started to warn her, but she interrupted him.

"No, I know. I know you like to boss me around and you know I love it. I'm just saying, you don't have to tell me to hold back. I'm not going to. I swear."

At Cookie's choked laughter, Dude explained to his friends. "It's the drugs, she says whatever she's thinking, with no filters."

"Obviously," Cookie observed, still smiling.

"Faulkner?" Cheyenne asked, sounding completely out of it.

"Yes, Shy?" Dude didn't look up from what between her legs.

"I do love you, you know. I was trying to figure out when to tell you, but the longer I waited, the harder it was to find the best time. I was going to make you dinner one night, but forgot I had to work, and besides I'm a shitty cook. Then I was going to tell you when you had me on my knees for you, but that didn't seem right either, and besides it wasn't as if I could really talk with my mouth full anyway. Then I was going to wait until you untied me that one night...God that was hot...but anyway, I fell asleep too soon. It didn't seem right to just blurt it out...but I do. I love you so much. You're everything I ever wanted in a guy. In *my* guy. I never knew I wanted to submit, but you make it so easy. I-I-I don't know what I'll do if you decide you don't want me anymore."

Dude paused for a fraction, he had to respond to the pain he heard in her voice. "Shy..."

"No! I know, I'm probably fucking this up somehow. I feel like I'm floating, but I just, I'd do anything for you. You have to know. I'll even leave you alone if you want me to. It might kill me, but I'll do it."

"I'm not letting you go, Shy."

"Oh. Okay. Good. 'Cos I like you holding me."

Dude shook his head and concentrated on the device again. "Fuck," he said quietly. "Cookie, Benny, stop. They've connected the three bombs to each other. I can't disarm this one without disarming the others at the same time."

Never one to let an opportunity to rub something in go by, Cookie said, "Looks like you needed both of us here after all, didn't you?"

"Fucker," Dude said lightly, knowing Cookie was right. There was no way he could disarm all three bombs at the same time. He needed both his teammates there.

"Hunter?"

"Yeah, Cheyenne?"

"How's Fiona? I bet she was really worried. And she didn't see Javier did she? I don't want her freaked out. I know she's still dealing with those assholes from Mexico kidnapping her. Not that Javier got her, but still. I'm worried about her. I miss her. We didn't get to finish our shots…"

"She's okay, Cheyenne, don't worry about her."

"Yeah, all right, she has you. I'll try not to. But I've never had best friends before. That's what friends do, they worry about each other."

There was silence as the three men continued to try to remove enough tape to safely get to the bombs underneath. Every time they had to peel some of the tape away from her skin they cringed. The red blotches underneath the tape looked bad.

"Okay, the first two are uncovered, how're you doing up there Benny?" Dude asked urgently. Time was ticking away. Too much time. He wasn't going to get a second chance.

"Almost done, Dude."

"Kason...I like that name. Why do you go by Benny?"

Benny opened his mouth, but Cookie answered before he could.

"He earned his nickname fair and square, Cheyenne. No matter if he says differently."

"Ooooooooh, I sense a good story there," Cheyenne slurred. "Can you see my arm guys? Is it still attached? I can't feel it at all. That can't be good can it? Faulkner?"

"Yeah, baby?"

"I love you."

"I know."

"Aren't you going to say it back?"

"Yeah, when you're out of this fucking building and I have you safe in my arms in my bed and you've just come for me three times and I'm sure you'll never be in this kind of fucked up situation again."

"Uh, Faulkner?"

"What?" Dude's voice was all business. As much as he loved Cheyenne, he was trying to concentrate.

"That was a lot of swear words, but I can't wait."

Dude blew out a breath, but didn't answer her.

"Okay guys, here's what I need you to do. See that little red wire running under the device? On the count of three you need to pull it out. Pull it as hard as you can. It has to pop out. We have to do it at the same time. If we don't, they'll all go off."

"Oh God, don't. Please don't." Cheyenne said suddenly, she started squirming under them, and Benny put both hands on her shoulders to try to keep her still. Dude hadn't been sure she was understanding what they were doing, but with her words he knew she did. She knew exactly. "Just leave it, fuck. Don't. Kason, Hunter, just go, take Faulkner with you. Don't." She started trembling hard.

Dude checked his watch. He had time, barely, but he had time. He moved up to Cheyenne's line of vision. He sandwiched her head between his hands and leaned down to her.

"Cheyenne, stop it."

She stopped moving, but he saw tears falling from her eyes for the first time since they'd arrived. She'd been so strong, but when it got too real, she finally broke.

"I can't. I want to touch you, Faulkner, and I can't. I've never been so scared in my life, not for me, but for *you*. I can't be the reason Fiona loses her man. I can't be the reason Benny never meets the woman who's out there waiting for him to protect her. I can't be the reason you die. If I die, it'll be okay, you'll find someone else, but I can't kill you. Please, Faulkner, please."

Dude could feel his heart breaking. He leaned down and kissed the tears falling from her right eye, then did the same on the left side.

"Shy, I'll never find anyone else. Ever. You're it. Period. Done. End of story. I've waited for you my entire life. If I have to go a day without tasting what flavor lip shit you've put on, I won't survive. If I can't see you night after night stretched out on my bed, waiting for me to come to you and do whatever I want, if I can't feel you surrounding me, squeezing me, my life isn't worth living." Dude's voice dropped to a whisper. "I love you, Shy. We're in this together. Okay?"

"You don't *ask* me stuff, Faulkner."

"Sorry." Dude held back the chuckle. She was so fucking cute even covered in tape. "I love you, Shy. We're in this together."

Cheyenne sniffed. "Can you please wipe my nose? I can't get to it and I can't stand feeling snot run down my face."

Dude smiled and used his sleeve to wipe the errant tears off her face then to clear the fluid away from her face that had leaked out of her nose.

"Can I please disarm this fucking bomb and get us out of here now?"

Cheyenne nodded.

Dude leaned down one more time and kissed her lips. "Hang in there, this is almost done."

He moved back down her body to the device between her knees.

"Is Summer okay? I mean Alicia and Javier left the camera thingy for me to watch. I think they were wanting me to have to watch you guys get blown up or something, but you're way too smart for that aren't you? Anyway, I heard Alicia…"

"On the count of three. One…"

"…shoot. Twice! And she told me she shot Summer, and I wasn't sure if she was dead or not, but I saw you guys carry her out and she was holding on to Sam, so I thought she looked okay and you guys weren't freaking out or anything. But it was awful. Is she…"

"Two…"

"…okay? I mean it couldn't have been fun to have been kidnapped, *again*. Fuckers. And Caroline? Is she okay? I mean it had to have sucked to have been sitting in *Aces* and to find out we were missing. Where are Fiona and Caroline? Is someone watching…"

"Three!"

"…them because Alicia and Javier know who they are and are still out there. They're planning on flying out of the country. Did you guys know that? They told me…stupid jerks, so you should be sure…"

"Cheyenne."

"…to track them down before they get out of the country. Can we steal them back if they go to Mexico? I can never remember all the rules about that sort of thing. I want to go out again with the girls. Next week. No tomorrow. We didn't get…"

"Cheyenne."

"…to finish our girl's night out and that was the first girls night out I've ever had. I was having fun dammit. It's not fair. It wasn't our fault stupid people had to go and ruin it…"

Cheyenne's words were suddenly cut off. She looked up to see Faulkner kneeling by her side and saw Kason and Hunter standing above her.

"It's over, Shy."

"You turned the bombs off?"

Dude smiled at her wording. "Yeah, we turned them off."

"Can we go home now, Faulkner? I want to sleep for a million hours in your bed. With you. Naked. Preferably with you inside me."

"Soon. First I need to get you to the hospital."

"But Faulkner, I don't wanna go to the hospital. I just want to be with you."

"You'll be with me, Shy. I'm not leaving your side and I want to see anyone *try* to peel me away."

"Okay then, but soon? You'll take me to bed?"

"Yes, Shy. Soon."

Looking up at Hunter and Kason, and seeing the broad grins on their faces, Cheyenne demanded, "What's so funny? I don't think there's anything funny about any of this." Her eyes went back to Faulkner. "Tell them to stop laughing."

"You're so fucking cute, Shy."

"No, I'm not," she retorted immediately. "I haven't been able to put on my lip balm in hours, my lips don't taste like anything, and I want to make sure they always taste like something different so you want to keep kissing me. I'm covered in fucking tape, *again*, but this time I know it's gonna hurt like hell when they take it off. I have no idea how they're going to get it out of my hair without cutting it all fucking off. I can't feel my arm and I'm afraid they're going to have to cut that off too. I'm just so tired of being scared and now I'm going to cry again and I still can't wipe my own snot off my face."

Dude leaned down and lifted Cheyenne into his arms. "Wipe your snot on me, Shy, I can handle it. I swear to Christ you aren't going to feel anything when they take the tape off, they aren't going to cut your hair off and you'll still have your arm when you wake up."

Dude felt Cheyenne nod against his shoulder where she'd buried her head and then wiped her face on his shirt, obviously taking him at his word and wiping her face on him to stop her snot from running down her face. He smiled.

"And another thing, I want to kiss you no matter if you're wearing flavored lip crap or not."

"Okay. I want to hold you."

"You will. Just shush now. Let me take care of you."

"You always take care of me."

"Damn straight."

Chapter Seventeen

CHEYENNE GROANED AND opened her eyes. The room was dark, but she knew immediately she was at the hospital. There was no mistaking the smell of antiseptic, old person, and sickness. Feeling panicky, she looked to her right and sighed.

Faulkner was there. She remembered bits and pieces of the last few hours, and he'd kept his word and not left her side. He'd carried her out of the basement into the bright sunlight of the day. There had been cameras and people yelling for information, but Faulkner had ignored all of them and his teammates had escorted him, shielding them from the cameras, to the waiting ambulance. He hadn't left her there this time though, he'd sat at her head and kept his scarred hand on her forehead the entire trip.

The emergency room had been expecting them and Cheyenne had been whisked to the back behind a flimsy curtain. A doctor had come in, almost immediately, and taken stock. Cheyenne didn't remember much after that, only that she'd been given another shot and in panic had looked to Faulkner.

He'd dipped his head to hers and whispered, "Trust me."

She'd nodded and was out.

Cheyenne watched as Faulkner breathed in and out. The rhythm of his breaths were steady and even. She'd watched him sleep enough to know he was sleeping deeply instead of the light cat-naps he was wont to do here and there.

She swore under her breath when the door opened and Faulkner jerked awake. He probably needed the sleep and it'd just been rudely interrupted. Cheyenne kept her eyes on Faulkner and was rewarded with his bright smile when he saw she was awake.

He stood up and came over to her side. "Hey, Shy. How do you feel?"

"Terrible." Her voice croaked a bit but she was honest, as usual.

Faulkner actually chuckled at her answer. She frowned at him.

"Give it a bit of time, Cheyenne, you'll feel better soon."

Cheyenne turned to see a man standing by her bed. She didn't recognize him, but he was obviously her doctor.

"We were able to remove most of the tape without

pulling off your skin this time. It'll take a bit of time for the hair on your arms and legs to grow back though."

Cheyenne remembered for the first time how the tape had covered her head. She moved her good arm up as if to feel for herself if she was indeed bald, but Faulkner intercepted it and kissed her palm before engulfing it in his own scarred hand.

"My hair?"

"That was a bit more problematic. Your man here," the doctor gestured at Faulkner, "refused to let us shave it, but we did have to cut some of it to get the tape out."

Tears gathered in the corners of Cheyenne eyes, but she refused to let them fall. It was stupid to cry over something like that. She was alive, Faulkner was alive, her friends were alive. Her hair would grow back.

"It looks fine, Shy," Falkner whispered in her ear. "It's just shorter than it was. Trust me."

Damn him for continuing to say that. She *did* trust him, but it was still scary not to see for herself. She bit her lip, then nodded at Faulkner. The smile that came over his face was all the reward Cheyenne needed. She'd walk through fire in order to see him smile at her like that. To know she pleased him.

The doctor continued speaking, "Your shoulder is going to take a bit longer to heal. You were lucky in that it was only a subluxation." At the blank look in Cheyenne's face, the doctor explained, "Sorry, that means it was only a partial dislocation. We didn't have to do surgery to put it back in place, we just manipulated it here in the ER. That doesn't mean it's not going to hurt. We want to watch you carefully since it was dislocated for a long period of time. You'll need to baby it for a while. There are some studies that show keeping it in a sling doesn't really help it much, so just do what you can and be careful. If the sling helps, use it. If you get tired and need to take a break from it, do so. I've written out a prescription for some painkillers. I recommend that you use them for the first day or so, then you can wean yourself off of them."

"No drugs," Cheyenne insisted. "I hate the way they make me feel."

Dude chuckled from beside her. "I have to agree with her in this. They really make her not herself, but I know if I ever need any information out of her, how to get it."

"That's not funny, Faulkner," Cheyenne chided him.

"But it's true."

Ignoring Faulkner for the moment, Cheyenne turned back to the doctor. "When can I go home?"

"Today."

Cheyenne sighed in relief.

"We have to get the paperwork in order and put you on the list for discharge, but you should be on your way in a couple of hours."

Faulkner stuck his hand out for the doctor to shake. "Thanks for everything, Doc. I mean it."

"You're welcome." He shook Faulkner's hand then turned back to Cheyenne.

"You're a very lucky lady, Cheyenne. You have quite the champion here. He wouldn't leave your side and insisted on overseeing the removal of all that tape. I wouldn't let him slip out of your grasp."

Cheyenne looked up at Faulkner and smiled. "No way, he's mine and I'm not letting him go."

CHEYENNE WAS DOZING on the bed, waiting for the doctor to come back and give them the all clear. She was ready to get out of there.

She heard Faulkner say, "What the hell?" and she opened her eyes to see her mom and sister walk into her room.

"No, hell no. You aren't staying."

"Uh, we're here to see my daughter," Cheyenne's mom said hesitantly.

"No you're not, you're here to upset her," Faulkner retorted.

"Cheyenne, really. Who is this?" Karen sneered. "He obviously doesn't have any manners. Should I call security to have him removed, Mother?"

Before Faulkner could say anything, Cheyenne spoke up. "Please, Karen, by all means, call security, but it'll be to remove the two of you and not Faulkner."

"Really Cheyenne, seriously. We've talked about this, you have to stop being a drama queen."

"Why are you here?" Cheyenne asked, trying to scoot up in the bed.

Faulkner leaned over and helped her into a sitting position, Cheyenne spared him a quick smile in thanks before turning her attention back to her family.

"We're here because you're family," her mom said, somehow sounding bored.

"Are you?" Cheyenne heard Faulkner growl from beside her. She put her hand on his and squeezed. She was thankful he was there, but she had to handle this herself.

"Of course we are! She's my daughter and Karen's sister."

The silence in the room grew awkward. Cheyenne refused to break it. If they were here for a reason, they'd get to it soon enough.

"We saw on the news that you were kidnapped again."

Cheyenne waited for her sister to get to the point.

"Seriously, it seems like your job is obviously putting you in danger, if you'd just find something a lot less dangerous, this wouldn't keep happening to you."

Cheyenne squeezed Faulkner's hand as hard as she could. She could feel every muscle in his body tense at her sister's words.

"How exactly is it my fault I got attacked when I was grocery shopping, Karen? And how exactly is it my fault that the 'poor family,' as you called them, if I recall correctly, felt the need to avenge their brothers and come after me? My job had nothing to do with this. I sit in a room and answer a telephone. That's it."

"But, Cheyenne, look at your sister," her mom spoke up, obviously once again supporting Karen and not bothering to think about how much her words could hurt her other daughter. "She works for the justice system, she helps put bad guys behind bars, you just answer a phone."

"Mom, she doesn't put bad guys behind bars, the lawyers do. She answers phones and does all the dirty work for the lawyers who do the real work. How is her job any different from mine?"

"I'm fucking done with this," Dude couldn't keep quiet anymore. "Your daughter doesn't 'just answer phones,' she is the lifeline for people who call needing help. Sometimes she's the only thing between someone living and dying. She walks people through first aid, she gives comfort, she helps bring the police and paramedics to people who need it. She's on the front lines every day working her ass off with no thanks and no rewards for it. There's no 'just' about anything Cheyenne does. I'm fucking proud of her for what she does, but that's not the fucking point here. As her *family*, you should've been at her side last night when she was brought in. You should be proud of her because she's your flesh and blood, not because of what she does for a living. You should be ashamed of yourselves."

Dude heard both women gasp, but he continued.

"Cheyenne also told me she disowned you both because of the way you acted the last time you saw her. That means she's done with you. *Done.* If she decides she wants to give you another chance, that's up to her. Not you. She probably will, because she's a big softy, but I'll tell you this right now, if you ever disparage her again, you'll never have another chance to talk to her. I'll bar you from her life. I won't allow her to be talked down to and I won't allow you to hurt her any more than you already have. So leave. Both of you. Think about what you're losing. If you don't care, that's on you, not Cheyenne."

Cheyenne watched as Karen's lips tightened. "Come on, Mother, if Cheyenne wants to hang out with this low-life, let her."

Her mom took another look at Cheyenne and turned to follow her daughter out of the room without a word.

Dude put his thumb against Cheyenne's chin and

turned her face toward him. He looked into her eyes for a moment then sighed. "I'm sorry, Shy. Not sorry I told them off, but sorry you had to deal with that today of all days. Don't listen to a word they say. You're amazing. What you do is amazing. I'm crazy about every inch of you."

"Thank you, Faulkner. I'm glad you were here."

"You didn't need me here, you held your own just fine, but I'm glad I was here too."

Putting her so-called family behind her once and for all, Cheyenne knew they wouldn't change. She'd lived her entire life trying to please them and hadn't gotten anywhere. She'd probably cry about it later, in Faulkner's arms, but for now she was over it.

"Can you check with the doctor and see how much longer it'll be until we can leave?"

"Of course. I'll be right back."

"I'm okay. Really."

"I know you are, Shy. I love you."

Cheyenne smiled as Faulkner opened the door and checked the hallway for any sign of her family. Obviously not seeing them, he smiled back at her then closed the door behind him.

Cheyenne snuggled down into the bed, sliding her butt back down until she was lying flat again, and closed her eyes. Maybe she'd just take a short nap while she wanted for Faulkner to get back and get her out of here.

CHEYENNE SETTLED INTO the seat of Faulkner's truck with a sigh. She was so glad to get out of the hospital it wasn't funny. They'd exited through the back exit because, unfortunately, the media had camped out at the front doors. The entire story of her re-kidnapping and the subsequent bomb threat to her, as well as to an entire city block, was huge news. Not to mention the fact that the abductors were related to the men who'd done the same thing a few months back.

Cheyenne knew Faulkner wouldn't let them get anywhere near her, and it allowed her to relax. He'd take care of her.

"Are you up to a short stop on the way home, Shy?"

Cheyenne looked over at Faulkner. He looked rumpled and tired, but she'd stop wherever he needed to with no questions. It didn't matter that she was wearing another pair of borrowed scrubs and desperately wanted a shower. If Faulkner wanted to stop somewhere, she was okay with it.

"Of course. Stop wherever you need to. I'm fine."

Dude leaned over and tagged Shy behind the neck and drew her to him gently, careful not to jostle her shoulder. "You *are* fine. And thank you."

He let her go and started the truck. "I need to tell you something before we get home. You'll find out soon enough, but I wanted to give you some warning."

"What?" Cheyenne asked suspiciously.

"You're moving in with me."

"What? Faulkner! You can't ask that already, it's too soon!"

"I'm not asking, Shy. Remember? You told me that when we were in the basement of that damn building. I don't ask. I tell."

"Well, yeah, I kinda remember that, but Faulkner, this is soon."

"It is, but you love me. I love you. I'll never love anyone else. I'll never let you love anyone else. So you're moving in. We might as well start the rest of our life now. We've missed enough time together. I'm not letting you spend another damn night in anyone's bed but mine."

Cheyenne felt her insides melt. She pressed her lips together and tried not to cry. "I never thought I'd be here."

"Where?"

"Here. With you. In a relationship where I'd feel comfortable enough to let someone make these kinds of decision for me. Where I didn't have to worry about having a bad day at work, knowing I'd have someone who'd listen to me and comfort me. Where I didn't have to compete for affection. Where I didn't have to justify my actions to someone. I never thought I'd be this happy, Faulkner."

"I can't promise it'll all be sunshine and roses, Shy."

"I never asked for that. I'm not an idiot. I work weird hours. You're in the military. You're a SEAL. I know you'll be sent off to do something I can't ask about and will never know about. But you know what? You'll come back to me. I couldn't have lived through…hell, *we* couldn't have lived through what we did to have it taken from us now. When you have to go, I'll cry, I'll pout, I'll be sad. But I'll hang out with the girls. We'll drink too much in the safety of someone's house, I'll go to work, I'll continue on until you come home. Then you'll boss me around, deny me orgasms, then give them to me over and over again until you're satisfied. Then you'll fuck me until we're both noodles, then we'll do it all again. And I'll love every second of it."

Dude smiled over at Cheyenne. "I love you."

"I'm not done."

"Sorry, Shy, by all means, continue."

Cheyenne smiled at her man. Fuck she loved him. "I figured something out. And once I did, I got it."

"What'd you figure out?"

"I figured out that when and if you get mad at me it's not because you're necessarily *mad* at me. It's because you're worried about me." She paused a fraction then continued. "And I know you told me this, but I didn't *really* get it. That day on the beach, when I was scared to call you because I was afraid you'd be mad…it's because my sister would get mad at me. She'd get furious and scream at me. She scared me and that's what I understood anger to be. But then I saw it with Fiona and Hunter. We went to a movie and she forgot to text him. When she did finally get in touch with him, he yelled and ranted and raved, but through it all, Fiona was stoic. She wasn't afraid of him. When he was done he hugged her so hard I thought her ribs would break.

"He was worried about her. He was mad because he thought she had a flashback. He didn't know where she was and he thought she could be in trouble. I got it. So I don't want you to ever be afraid to yell at me. I know you won't hurt me, and I know you're mad because you care about me, because you're worried. I get it now."

Dude had to pull the truck over. Jesus. He pulled into a parking lot of a business that was right off the road. He put the truck in gear and opened his door. He strode around until he got to the passenger side. He opened the door and immediately leaned in, resting both hands on the seat next to Cheyenne.

"Shy, I swear to God, you have to stop doing this to me when I'm driving." Dude smiled at her then moved so his hands on her thighs. "I love you. I love you so much it scares the living hell out of me. I worry about you all the time. All the fucking time. You could be in the other room and I worry if you're okay. Are you hungry? Cold? Happy? Sad? Content? I have a feeling you're going to see me 'mad' a lot. I'm thrilled to pieces you told me, but know that I'm going to do everything I can to not yell at you or get mad. I don't want you to lose your independence. Hell, I love that about you, but you have to promise to keep me updated about where you are and when you might be getting home.

"Text me, call me, leave me a note, whatever it takes, just tell me. You want to go out for lunch? No problem. Text me. You want to go shopping with the girls? Great. Spend all the fucking money you want, but tell me that's where you'll be. If you're stopping to get gas before coming home? Let me know. Because I swear if you're two minutes late I'm going to worry. I'm not being controlling, I'm not being an asshole. I'm *worrying* about you. I can't handle you being taken out from under my nose again. I swear I can't. If I don't know where you are for five minutes I'm likely to call the team and track your ass down."

Cheyenne put her good hand on Faulkner's cheek. "I promise."

"Oh and you should probably know, you and all the other girls will have fucking tracking devices on just about everything you own."

"What?"

"Yeah, we worked with Tex and he's ordering them and will set up the software."

"Uh, that's a bit over the top, Faulkner."

"No, it isn't. Caroline was taken by an FBI traitor and hauled out into the middle of the ocean so they could dispose of her body. Alabama was living on the fucking streets and no one could find her. Fiona was taken into a foreign fucking country and about to be sold as a sex slave and Summer was kidnapped by a murderous, bastard, pedophile rapist. And you, you had three fucking goddamn bombs strapped to you and were hidden in the basement of an apartment building. It's not over the fucking top at all."

"You're swearing a lot, Faulkner."

Dude just shook his head and dropped it to his chest and closed his eyes for a moment, trying to get himself back under control. Figures that instead of bitching about the fact he'd just ordered tracking devices so he'd be able to find her no matter what she was wearing, carrying, or where she was going, Cheyenne concentrated on his language.

Dude lifted his head up again and leaned in to kiss her. He took Cheyenne's lips in a hard, deep kiss then drew back and smiled. "I can't place it."

"Pomegranate."

Dude just shook his head and ran his tongue over his lips. "Delicious."

He kissed Cheyenne on the forehead then backed up and closed her door. He jogged back around to his side and jumped in. "Okay, we're going to be late, I'll just blame you and your penchant for wearing flavored lip crap."

"Okay," Cheyenne agreed with a smile, not knowing what they were going to be late for, but not caring either.

Dude drove until they pulled into a familiar parking lot. Cheyenne beamed at him.

"Are you serious?"

"I figured since you bitched so much about not getting to finish your girl's night out, that there was no time like the present. Although, you'll have to deal with it being a friend's night out instead. Everyone's inside waiting on us."

"Thank you, Faulkner. I love you."

"I love you too, Shy. But don't think I've forgotten about you not saying the words until we were in a life and death situation. I owe you for that."

"I'm sure you'll make me pay...tonight."

"Damn straight I will. When we get home I'll help you remove your clothes and get you situated on our bed. I can't tie your arms, but I'll tie your legs until you're spread eagled and can't close them. You'll not touch me and not move an inch while I take my fill of you. You won't be allowed to come until I say, and Shy, I'm pissed you made me wait to hear you say it."

Cheyenne smiled, his words said he was pissed, but

the carnal look in his eyes said otherwise.

"Then I'll take you hard, while you're still tied, and see how many times I can make you explode before I fill you up."

Cheyenne's ears rang and she could feel her own harsh breathing.

"Do we have to go inside?"

"Yes. And you'll not drink anything alcoholic. You still probably have some morphine in your system and I won't chance it. You can have orange juice, but no soda, your body needs nutrients, not crap right now."

"Okay, Faulkner."

"When I say it's time to go, we're going. Don't argue with me. I know you're probably more tired than you're letting on. And your shoulder probably hurts too. That over-the-counter painkiller probably isn't cutting it. But I wanted to give you this, Shy. I'll give you anything and everything you want if it's in my power."

"Okay, Faulkner."

"I love you, Shy."

"I love you too."

"Okay, let's do this so I can go and welcome you to your new home."

"Our new home."

"Yeah, *our* new home."

Epilogue

T HE LARGE GROUP of friends sat at the table at *Aces*. Cheyenne, Summer, and Alabama had insisted on coming back to the bar at the first opportunity. Their men, of course, wanted to boycott the place altogether and never set foot in it again, but the women put their foot down.

"I won't allow those jerks to run us out of the best bar in town. We love this place." Summer had argued with Mozart until she was blue in the face, and he, as well as Dude and Abe had still refused.

They'd only given in when the women made plans to go back on their own. Of course that made all the men change their minds in a heartbeat. They wouldn't let them go back without them.

The moment Cheyenne stepped inside *Aces*, she'd frozen, but Faulkner was right there at her back. He put his arms around her and pulled back into his hard body. They'd stood in the middle of the entrance, not moving. Faulkner leaned down and whispered in her ear. Cheyenne could feel the breath from his words tickling her ear.

"You can do this, Shy. You're not alone. You just stand here as long as you need to. I'm here."

His words gave Cheyenne the strength to take a deep breath. She intertwined her fingers with Faulkner's, rubbing her thumb over the stubs of his fingers for a second, then she turned in his arms and laid her head on his chest, wrapping her arms as far around his back as she could without hurting her shoulder.

"Thank you, Faulkner. I love you."

"I love you too, Shy. Come on, let's get a drink."

After that, entering *Aces* became easier. It had gotten to a point where Cheyenne and the other women would meet up at the little bar at least once a week. Sometimes they'd be by themselves and other times they'd go with their men.

The men also still went there to unwind as well, with their women's blessing. Typically they'd have a women's night in and a men's night out at the same time. The men could go out and have a beer or two, and the women would hole up in Caroline's house and do whatever it was that women did when they got together.

Three months had gone by since the women had been kidnapped and for once, everything had been quiet. The team had left twice on missions, but they were short and they hadn't been out of the country for more than four days for each one.

The team sat around the table nursing their beers and Cookie laughed when he caught Dude looking at his watch for the third time in the last twenty minutes.

"Suck it up, Dude, seriously, you can go one night without ordering Cheyenne to service you." Cookie said the words softly, for Dude's ears only, wanting to tease him, but not wanting to share his secret.

"Shut it, Cookie, I warned you not to spread that shit around. I know you heard what Cheyenne said in that basement, but that stays between the three of us."

"Don't worry, Dude, I might tease you about it, but I'd never break your, or her, confidence that way."

Dude just snorted. Cheyenne had left for her shift that afternoon and he'd taken her hard that morning. She was always willing to do whatever he wanted to try, and that morning he'd gotten creative. Dude had blindfolded her, tied her hands behind her back, and played with her back passage for the first time before taking her hard. Dude loved that Cheyenne trusted him enough to try things she wasn't sure about. Their lovemaking that morning took the ultimate trust, and Cheyenne had not only tolerated him making love to her in a new way, but if her moans were any indication, she'd enjoyed it and wanted more.

The waitress, Jess, limped up to the table and put another round of beers on the table. She turned to leave without her usual friendly conversation.

Benny grabbed a hold of her upper arm as she turned to go. "Hey, Jess, how've you been? Haven't see you around lately."

Benny, and the other men frowned at the grimace that came over the waitress's face. Benny quickly let go of her arm and she stepped back a foot and glanced at the men around the table then back down to the tray she was holding in her hands.

"Uh, yeah, I've had some stuff going on at home."

"Everything okay?" Benny asked, not liking how she'd flinched from him. He wasn't the biggest man around the table, but he wasn't exactly small. He knew he could be scary, but Jess *knew* him. She knew all of them. She'd been serving them all for a while now.

"Yeah." Her tone was flat, and while not unfriendly, it wasn't inviting further conversation, which was unusual for her.

Benny watched as she glanced around the room furtively and then simply turned away from the table and limped with her funny little gait, back to the bar.

"That wasn't normal," Dude commented unnecessarily.

"No shit." Benny returned, his eyes not leaving the waitress as she gathered another set of drinks from the bar.

Dude watched as Benny took a deep breath and

turned back to the group. They could tell he didn't want to let the odd encounter with the waitress go, but he did anyway. The conversation turned back to their normal friendly chatter until finally Benny was the first to call it a night.

"I know you guys all have women to get back to, and I should be the last one to leave, but I'm just not in the mood anymore. Say hey to all your women for me. I'll see you at PT."

Dude and the rest of the team watched their friend leave. They were worried about him. Benny was now the odd-man out. The only man on the team that didn't have a woman to worry about, to love. They couldn't lose him. They might pick on him, but Benny was an important part of their team. No one wanted to see him put in transfer paperwork to another SEAL team.

After Benny left, the rest of the guys decided they might as well call it a night too. They all had women waiting for them. Dude's thoughts turned back to Cheyenne. He looked at his watch. Perfect. Eleven. She'd switched to first shift and didn't have to work through the evening anymore. After work that afternoon she'd gone over to Caroline's house for dinner and to visit for a few hours.

Even though she'd been visiting with her friends, Dude had told her to leave around a quarter to eleven and head back to their house. He planned it so she'd arrive home just before he would, and he'd told her just how to be waiting for him. She always followed his instructions to the letter. He had a bag in the truck waiting with new toys he'd picked out just for her. Dude couldn't wait. He was the luckiest bastard alive.

Look for the next book in the
SEAL of Protection Series:
Protecting Jessyka.

Discover other titles by Susan Stoker

SEAL of Protection Series

Protecting Caroline

Protecting Alabama

Protecting Fiona

Marrying Caroline (novella)

Protecting Summer

Protecting Cheyenne

Protecting Jessyka

Protecting Julie (novella)

Protecting Melody

Protecting the Future

Delta Force Heroes Series

Rescuing Rayne

Assisting Aimee (loosely related to DF)

Rescuing Emily

Rescuing Harley

Rescuing Kassie (TBA)

Rescuing Casey (TBA)

Rescuing Wendy (TBA)

Rescuing Mary (TBA)

Badge of Honor: Texas Heroes Series

Justice for Mackenzie
Justice for Mickie
Justice for Corrie
Justice for Laine (novella)
Shelter for Elizabeth
Justice for Boone
Shelter for Adeline (TBA)
Justice for Sidney (TBA)
Shelter for Blythe (TBA)
Justice for Milena (TBA)
Shelter for Sophie (TBA)
Justice for Kinley (TBA)
Shelter for Promise (TBA)
Shelter for Koren (TBA)
Shelter for Penelope (TBA)

Beyond Reality Series

Outback Hearts
Flaming Hearts
Frozen Hearts

Writing as Annie George

Stepbrother Virgin (erotic novella)

Connect with Susan Online

Susan's Facebook Profile and Page:
www.facebook.com/authorsstoker
www.facebook.com/authorsusanstoker

Follow Susan on Twitter:
www.twitter.com/Susan_Stoker

Find Susan's Books on Goodreads:
www.goodreads.com/SusanStoker

Email: Susan@StokerAces.com

Website: www.StokerAces.com

To sign up for Susan's Newsletter go to:
http://bit.ly/SusanStokerNewsletter

Or text: STOKER to 24587 for text alerts on your mobile device

About the Author

New York Times, *USA Today,* and *Wall Street Journal* Bestselling Author Susan Stoker has a heart as big as the state of Texas, where she lives, but this all-American girl has also spent the last fourteen years living in Missouri, California, Colorado, and Indiana. She's married to a retired Army man who now gets to follow *her* around the country.

She debuted her first series in 2014 and quickly followed that up with the SEAL of Protection Series, which solidified her love of writing and creating stories readers can get lost in.

If you enjoyed this book, or any book, please consider leaving a review. It's appreciated by authors more than you'll know.

25090160R00163

Printed in Poland
by Amazon Fulfillment
Poland Sp. z o.o., Wrocław